NEVER STOP SMILING

"Let's do it!" Teresa purred. "Then we can let the judges decide who's prettier." She tore an entry form from the board and flashed a smug smile in Danielle's direction.

Danielle bristled. "As if your mother would ever let you be in a beauty contest."

"Oh, she'll be thrilled," Teresa replied. "She was Miss Merivale Country Club when she was my age. My parents will be no problem—and I'm perfectly willing to compete with you if you really insist on being humiliated."

"Okay. You're on." Danielle tore off an entry form for herself. The battle was on, and there was no turning back now. Danielle had to win that contest—even if it cost her one of her best friends!

Merivale Mall

NEVER STOP SMILING

by Jana Ellis

Troll Associates

Library of Congress Cataloging-in-Publication Data

Ellis, Jana.
   Never stop smiling / by Jana Ellis.
     p.   cm.—(Merivale mall; #4)
   Summary: Determined to outdo her friend Teresa, Danielle enters
the Miss Merivale Mall contest and uses all the means at her
disposal to make sure that she wins.
   ISBN 0-8167-1360-X (pbk.)
   [1. Contests—Fiction. 2. Friendship—Fiction. 3. High schools—
Fiction. 4. Schools—Fiction.] I. Title. II. Series: Ellis, Jana.
Merivale mall; #4.
PZ7.E472Ne 1989
[Fic]—dc19   88-12390

A TROLL BOOK, published by Troll Associates,
Mahwah, NJ 07430

10 9 8 7 6 5 4 3 2 1

NEVER STOP SMILING

CHAPTER ONE

I could just scream. . . .

Sixteen-year-old Danielle Sharp rolled her emerald eyes and tossed her fiery red hair over one shoulder. She had had just about enough of Teresa Woods—even if Teresa was one of her best friends! All morning, while they'd been shopping with their other best friend, raven-haired Heather Barron, Teresa had been on one big ego-trip. It was enough to ruin Danielle's day. But then, not being the center of attention was always excruciating for Danielle.

It seemed every word out of Teresa's perfectly shaped mouth was designed to show just how fantastic she was, in every way. And of course, it was all true. A stunning brunette with thick shoulder-length hair and chocolate-colored eyes, Teresa Woods had everything—

fabulous looks, tremendous style, incredible breeding, and tons of money. She was truly elite.

But sitting at the mall on one of the stone benches, running on about how great she was, made her seem so boring, thought Danielle. It made it hard to remember that getting to be Teresa's friend had been one of Danielle's biggest victories.

When Danielle had first transferred to prestigious Atwood Academy as a freshman, she realized right away that Teresa Woods and Heather Barron were *the* girls to get to know—they were the absolute heart of the inner circle.

It took some conniving on Danielle's part, but finally one day Teresa had allowed her in. She invited Danielle to go shopping after school. After that, Heather Barron followed, and suddenly Danielle was in with everybody who mattered at Atwood—even Ashley Shepard and Wendy Carter, who had refused to *look* at her before.

This year Danielle and Teresa and Heather were the ruling threesome of the junior class in-crowd—or the Atwood Aristocracy, as they liked to call themselves. They were the all-around best—the most popular *and* the prettiest girls at Atwood.

Danielle, perhaps, was the flashiest and most

glamorous of the three, with her red hair, green eyes, and long, shapely legs.

But Teresa was beautiful by anybody's standards too. For starters, her eyes could melt a glacier. Then, there was that little rich girl pout of hers that made everybody in the entire world want to please her.

As for Heather, her blue black hair and ice blue eyes were a hard-to-beat combination, especially when she set them off with the expensive silver jewelry that was her trademark.

Normally, nothing was more fun for Danielle than a shopping excursion with Teresa and Heather. They'd stroll through Merivale Mall's most exclusive shops, trying on clothes—their favorite indoor sport—and buying whatever caught their eyes. They'd test cologne, scout for good-looking guys, fool around at makeup counters, all the time gossiping and laughing about other people—taking them apart was so-o much fun.

Then, to top it off, they'd indulge in some fantastic treat—such as the praline cones they were licking now as they sat outside The Big Scoop Ice Cream Parlor on the mall's first level.

"See? Praline is spectacular," said Teresa. "Remember that flavor you made us order the other day, Danielle? Mint chip?"

It wasn't *what* Teresa said, it was *how* she said it. A definite put-down.

"Yes. Mint chip," replied Danielle. "*I* thought it was terrific."

"It was okay," Heather tossed in, in her usual bored tone.

Thanks a lot, thought Danielle. It looked as if Heather wouldn't give her an inch that day either.

"So, anyway,"—Teresa was back to herself again—"I told him I wanted a great cut—no matter what it cost—"

Ugh, another reminder that Teresa had gobs and gobs of money. It was *super* irritating. Teresa *knew* Danielle was on an allowance—a huge one, but still an allowance—and she *knew* Danielle couldn't afford the Manor these days. To the Manor Born was the most expensive beauty salon in Merivale—no one got out of there without spending at least a hundred dollars.

"Well, if your hair is great, it really doesn't matter where you get it cut," Danielle said, smiling sweetly and gently lifting her luxurious mane with her fingers. *There, that should keep her quiet.*

"Well, I guess you and I just have different definitions of great," Teresa said just as sweetly.

There it was again—another dig. But Danielle decided to let this one drop.

"Guess what, guys—" she began, her green

eyes sparkling, "I've started riding lessons!" *At last! Something interesting to talk about!*

"Oh, Danielle, I know you're going to love riding." Heather Barron's usual boredom gave way to enthusiasm when riding was mentioned. Heather had been riding since she could walk. Her father had a passion for Arabian racehorses.

"That's fantastic!" Teresa agreed. "Who's your teacher?"

Danielle was about to answer when Teresa's face clouded over. "Oh, no. Not Saunders at Merivale Country Club—"

"Yes, Saunders."

"Oh, poor Dani." First Teresa cooed sympathetically, then she burst into giggles. "Those plaid shirts are too much, aren't they? I mean he must sleep in the stables with the horses. Honestly, you should try Jimmy Dixon at the Polo Club, Danielle. That's who *I* studied with when I was a beginner. Oh, and by the way, while you're calling to change riding teachers, give my hair stylist a call, okay?"

Danielle stared hard at the cone in her hand. "Oh? Is there a problem with my hair?"

"Well, as your friend, I have to be honest—" Teresa grimaced and shook her head hopelessly.

Danielle rolled her eyes at Heather as if to say, "Can you believe it?"

But Heather was looking around, wearing a

blank expression. She didn't seem to have even noticed.

"All I'm saying is, where you have your hair cut shows." Teresa was looking at Danielle with absolute pity now. "Remember that time I went to Snippers? That stylist wanted to henna my hair! I told him forget it. I would *never* go red in a million years! Red hair is so tacky. Oh, not *your* shade, Danielle, but, you know, *other* reds."

In her heart, Danielle understood that Teresa was just jealous of her. And she had lots of reason to be too! Danielle knew she was prettier, smarter, and just plain more popular. But even when she realized what the reason was, Danielle still felt rotten every time Teresa poked at her ego.

Danielle looked over at her friend, wishing the whole morning had never happened. "I think my hair looks just fine, Teresa." Danielle was making every effort to stay cool.

"Well, don't get all bent out of shape. Looks aren't everything, Danielle." Teresa threw her a brittle smile.

That was the last straw. Danielle's eyes flashed. She stood up and tossed the remains of her ice-cream cone into the trash basket as if it were a gauntlet.

"Since we're being honest, Teresa," Danielle began, looking at her friend with extreme pity, "the truth is, well, I am a lot better looking than you." Teresa just stared, openmouthed. "Ask anybody—anybody at all." Danielle daintily licked a bit of ice cream from her forefinger.

Heather Barron lowered her eyelids and gave her friends a sideways glance. "You're really ruining my good time, you know what I mean?" She tossed her empty cone in the garbage and wiped her hands on a white lace handkerchief. "I mean, really!"

"Well, maybe you can help us settle this once and for all, Heather, and then we'll leave you in peace," Teresa said, turning to her with a soft smile. "I know Danielle is kind of 'cute,' in a rustic sort of way, but wouldn't you say—just talking about looks now—that I have, well, a *slight* edge?" With that, Teresa lowered her super-long lashes and tried to look demure. When Heather didn't answer, she said, "Now, come on, spill it, who's got the right stuff?"

Heather smiled coyly and looked long and hard from one of her friends to the other. "It all depends on what you like, I guess," she finally said, thinking they could drop the subject now.

Teresa spoke up. "Don't be a wimp, Heather, be honest. Danielle's strong—she can take it."

"Forget it," said Heather, holding up her hand. "I'm not getting in the middle of this. If you want to compete, go join the Miss Merivale

Mall contest or something. I think it's totally weird for you to be fighting about your looks. I mean, think of all the *really* homely people walking around."

"You know, Heather's right," said Teresa. "It *is* silly for us to be fighting about this. And really, Danielle, you're not *that* bad looking. Your features are good, it's just what you *do* with them."

Danielle could feel herself exploding. All those times she had bent over backward to be nice to Teresa, all those knots she'd tied herself into, just to be accepted by her and her crowd. And this was how she paid Danielle back!

"I wish there was a Miss Merivale Mall contest, I really do." There was a challenge in Danielle's voice.

"I wasn't kidding. There's an announcement about it right over there. If you two weren't so busy discussing how beautiful you are, you'd have noticed it." Heather pointed to a sandwich board in the center of the promenade. "I wouldn't enter because I think beauty contests are tacky."

Danielle let Heather's dig roll off her and walked over to the poster and read. " 'First Annual Miss Merivale Mall Competition. Entrants must be under twenty-one years of age, residents of Merivale, unmarried. Winner will receive a scholarship grant and will be asked to host several promotional events.' "

Hmmmm— How perfect. If Teresa and I enter, Danielle thought, *I couldn't lose. Poor thing, she'd have to admit I'm prettier then.*

For starters, Danielle knew, Teresa would never have the nerve to compete. She knew that Danielle was the prettiest girl in Merivale.

Besides that, the Woods would never let Teresa enter a beauty contest. They were far too conservative.

"Heather, you're brilliant. You know, Teresa," Danielle mused, "I think you and I should enter this contest. I'd like a little competition. It'd make my win mean so much more." Danielle smiled like a cat; she felt very sure of herself.

But Teresa's reaction wasn't what Danielle expected. "Let's do it," she purred. "Then we can let the judges decide who's prettier." With that Teresa tore an entry form from the board and flashed a smug smile in Danielle's direction.

"As if your mother would ever let you be in a beauty contest."

"Oh, she'll be thrilled," was Teresa's withering reply. "She was Miss Merivale Country Club when she was my age. That's how she met my father. He was one of the judges. My parents will be no problem—and I'm perfectly willing to compete with you if you really insist on being humiliated."

Danielle sauntered over to the poster and slowly tore off an entry form for herself. She had always thought beauty contests were pretty dumb, but this one was an exception.

"Okay. You're on," she said coolly. Holding the form up between her thumb and forefinger, she gave it a gentle shake. Thank goodness there was nothing for Danielle to worry about—not really. Whatever Teresa had, Danielle had double. And red hair was so much more special than brown hair. Everybody knew that.

"I'm going home to fill this out immediately," Teresa announced suddenly. "Today's been a bust for shopping anyway. Want a lift, Heather?"

Heather looked at Danielle guiltily. "Has your 'Vette been fixed?" she asked Teresa.

Teresa smiled knowingly. "Yeah."

"Well, then I guess I have to ride with you. Bye, Danielle." Her decision made, Heather grabbed her bag and started off.

As they rounded the corner, Teresa turned back and waved tauntingly at Danielle. "May the prettier girl win."

Alone and smarting, Danielle watched them walk away. *If that's what you want, that's what you'll get.* The battle was on, and there was no turning back now. She had to win that contest—even if it cost her one of her best friends.

CHAPTER TWO

Left alone, Danielle took her first close look at the application form, and immediately realized she had a problem.

The ten finalists were to be chosen on the basis of a photograph and an essay. No problem with the photo, of course. From the time she had been a green-eyed baby girl gurgling in her playpen, Danielle Sharp had never taken a bad picture.

But the essay? How in the world could she write an essay about why she wanted to be Miss Merivale Mall?

Dear Judges, I want to be Miss Merivale Mall because I want to rub Teresa Woods's nose in the dirt. . . .

No, in this case, honesty was definitely not the best policy. If Danielle wanted to make the finals, she'd just have to write a terrific essay, one that would stand out from the rest. Something sincere, truthful, heartfelt, moving—impossible.

The sincere, heartfelt truth was that Danielle agreed with Heather and thought beauty contests were tacky, and essay writing was even worse.

Hmmm— If truthfulness and sincerity weren't going to make it, deviousness would have to do. Sitting down on the stone bench, Danielle asked herself, *Devious— Now what would Teresa Woods do at a time like this?*

Teresa's writing skills were pitiful, as everyone knew. So Teresa was probably out there right then, recruiting someone brilliant to write the essay for her. With all her family's clout, she could probably get Atwood's headmaster to write her essay.

Suddenly Danielle broke out in a smile. A big one this time. There was a way after all! There was somebody who could write an essay for her. An essay that was sincere, heartfelt, and truthful. Someone who would never say no to her either . . .

Feeling inside her soft suede bag to make sure she had her trusty Walkman with her, Danielle raced along the ground-level corridor— where the mall's cheapest shops were located.

She was heading for the tackiest sign of them all—the flashing orange of TIO'S TACOS.

It was a rare occasion when Danielle "lowered herself" to step inside a place like Tio's. If she ever did grace any ground-level establishment with her presence, it was only to get ice cream at The Big Scoop or cash at the bank. Once in a while she made an occasional foray into Video Arcade to check out the action.

But now it was for something even more important than money or boys. *Good old Cousin Lori to the rescue! She'll write my essay for sure!*

Of all the girls standing behind the counter at Tio's wearing orange nylon dresses with fluorescent yellow bib aprons, one stood out. Maybe it was because of her clear peaches-and-cream complexion.

Or maybe it was the pale flaxen hair that fell in a straight classic line and framed her face, or the intelligent blue eyes that darted from the customer to the counter as she packed an order of enchiladas to go.

Whatever it was, the girl was dazzling. And when she smiled there was no doubt whatsoever—the girl was someone special. Her name was Lori, Lori Randall—Danielle's first cousin and former best friend.

Lori and Danielle had been inseparable when

they were kids—more like sisters than cousins. But when Danielle's father made his fortune, the Sharps had moved to Wood Hollow Hills, Merivale's super-wealthy community, and the friendship had fizzled out—on Danielle's side at least.

And that had hurt Lori. But time had soothed the hurt, and Lori had other friends now. There was Patsy Donovan, a fellow junior at Merivale High, and countergirl at the Cookie Connection. And Ann Larson, also a junior at Merivale. She was a part-time aerobics teacher at the Body Shoppe, the mall's health spa.

But now—whenever she needed something— Danielle still came around. And Lori was always happy to see her. No matter what had happened between them, Lori still cared about Danielle.

"Well, hi there, stranger," said Lori, breaking into a genuine smile.

"Oh, Lori! It's so great to see you! You look fantastic!" Danielle looked smashing herself in her black designer slacks and a rust-colored angora sweater, the exact shade of her hair.

"What's up?" asked Lori. Danielle wasn't there for the food, Lori knew that much. The last time Danielle had breezed into Tio's with a big smile like the one she was wearing now, she had wanted a favor. She needed help minding some kids.

The time before that she had needed to borrow money—money that Lori had saved to buy her old, used, but beloved Spitfire. And though Danielle was late repaying it, she came through in the end, showing up at Lori's house with the car wrapped in a huge yellow ribbon. Danielle hadn't let her down.

"Gosh," Danielle gushed, "I really miss you, Lori. I haven't seen you in ages!" Danielle hoped she wasn't laying it on too thick.

She was—but Lori would never let on that she knew her cousin was up to something. Whenever Danielle showed up, a scheme was sure to follow. And from the energy Danielle was pouring out, Lori could tell this one was a biggie.

"Lori, I was just walking by and I saw you in here slaving away. I thought you could use a break. Come on—let's chat for a few minutes. I'll buy you a croissant, okay?"

A Super Biggie. "Well, I'll have to check first, Dani—" Turning, Lori called out, "Okay if I take my break now, Ernie?" Ernie Goldbloom was the "Tio" of Tio's Tacos.

The pudgy owner ran a hand over his balding head and smiled at his favorite employee. Lori was the kind of worker he could trust, the kind who didn't take advantage of a nice, lenient boss. "Sure, go ahead—"

Two minutes later Lori was seated on a stone bench beside Danielle, biting into a warm almond croissant.

"Well, nothing's new with me—same old stuff. Boys, cars, shopping. Let's talk about you! What have you been doing with yourself, other than working your tail off?"

"Oh, I've been working at my secret passion," Lori answered with a shy smile.

"Ooooo, sounds good! Secret passion, huh? I assume we are referring to Nick Hobart?" Nick was Lori's boyfriend, and the star quarterback at Atwood Academy. Any girl in town would love to date him, but Nick was crazy only about Lori.

Danielle could never figure out why a guy like Nick, who had all the important things— money, looks, a great bod—would want to go out with someone like Lori. Oh, she was pretty all right. But, for heaven's sake, she worked in an orange nylon dress.

"Not Nick." Lori giggled. "I meant designing. My art teacher thinks she can get me an appointment with this guy, Mr. Mortenson. He's a visiting professor from the Fashion Institute."

From the time Lori was about ten, she'd had a flair for art and design. She was hoping to turn a hobby into a potential career—one that would be exciting too!

Danielle stared at her cousin. "College is a year away! Isn't this a little premature?"

"Well, Mr. Mortenson's only going to be in Merivale for a day. He'll be one of the judges of the Miss Merivale Mall contest. If I don't get to see him while he's here, it means I have to take a trip to New York to be interviewed."

Miss Merivale Mall! How convenient! Danielle didn't even have to bring up the subject! "Miss Merivale Mall! Have you ever heard of anything so dumb in your entire life? I mean, why would *anyone* want to be Miss Merivale Mall?"

Danielle stared hard at her cousin. *Come on, Lori,* she urged silently, pressing the Record button on her Walkman. *Give me one of those straight-A essays of yours!*

"Well," began Lori, screwing up her forehead, "I don't have time to enter myself. I'm too busy working and getting my portfolio together—"

Lori was always slaving away. And it was a good thing too, Danielle thought. Her naturally beautiful cousin would have given Danielle her stiffest competition in the contest. "But if you did?"

"But if I did, I'd want to be Miss Merivale Mall because—because the mall is the heart and soul of the whole town, Danielle. It's the center of our community. It's a garden, it's a playground, it's a bazaar—a great place to meet people, to shop, to eat. It's got everything! To tell the truth, I can't imagine Merivale without the mall, Danielle. It's brought the whole town together—"

Danielle reached into her bag and shut off her Walkman.

"Well," she said. "Too bad you don't have time to enter, huh? Uh-oh. I forgot, I'm late for an appointment! See you around!"

With that, she sprang to her feet and kissed the air beside her cousin's cheek.

Running off down the promenade, Danielle made a tight fist of triumph with her right hand. *Thanks a billion, Cousin Lori,* she said to herself. *You just got me into the finals!*

Watching her cousin disappear, Lori wondered if she had misjudged Danielle. She didn't want anything from her after all. Just then a strong hand on her shoulder interrupted her thoughts.

"Nick!" Lori cried happily when she turned and saw her boyfriend.

"Hi, Lori. On a break?" Nick smiled at her, and the loving look in his blue green eyes made her knees turn to rubber and her heart race.

"Just for a few more minutes," said Lori, regaining her composure and smiling back.

Having part-time jobs right across the mall from each other was more than convenient, it was fantastic. Lori liked to think of the path between the two stores as a beam of good energy going from him to her and back again. Sometimes, when she was at the counter, she could see him, if he was in the VCR section of Hobart Electronics.

"I was just on my way to see if you wanted to take your break with me," Nick replied.

"Lori! Nick!" Down the mall, a girl with reddish brown hair and sparkling hazel eyes was walking toward them. On her head was a giant chocolate-chip cookie hat, the trademark of the Cookie Connection.

"Patsy!" Lori laughed. "What is this, a convention?"

"Hi, you two," said Patsy. .

Even in her absurd uniform, Patsy Donovan looked fantastic, mainly because she had a brand-new body. In the past few weeks Patsy had lost over thirty pounds.

Always a pretty girl, Patsy had been buried under a lot of extra weight. But now she had the potential to be a real knockout. All she needed was a little encouragement, and Lori and their friend, Ann Larson, gave her some every chance they could.

"I needed a break," Patsy confessed. "Those cookies were getting to me. I was just about to stuff a handful down my throat, so I told my supervisor I'd be back in ten minutes."

"I have to get back soon too," Nick said with a glance at his watch. "Lori, I wanted to ask you if you'd heard about the contest, and if you're going to enter. It's got incredible prizes."

"What contest?" Patsy interjected.

"You mean Miss Merivale Mall?" Lori said. "Nope. Too busy."

"They're having a contest for Miss Merivale Mall? Lori, you've *got* to enter—you'd win in a minute!"

"That's what *I* thought," Nick said, agreeing.

"Oh, sure, you guys." Lori laughed. "But I don't have time for my boyfriend"—she winked at Nick—"let alone extra time to be in a beauty contest! I've also got to put together a whole portfolio of my designs. One of the contest judges is Professor Mortenson of the Fashion Institute, and while he's here in Merivale, I've got to get him to look at my work." Lori took a thoughtful bite of her croissant.

"Mmm, that looks good," Patsy muttered hungrily. "I haven't pigged out in such a long time—"

"Speaking of time," Nick interrupted, kissing Lori tenderly on the forehead. "See you soon, Randall," he said.

"Not soon enough," Lori whispered, gazing up into his devastatingly gorgeous eyes.

"Bye, Patsy. Oh, by the way, you look great."

"Bye, Nick—" Patsy looked after him. "Boy, is he ever fantastic. You're so lucky, Lori—" She sighed sadly.

Lori was still looking after Nick, oblivious to Patsy's melancholy tone. Finally as Nick disappeared into his dad's store, Lori turned back to Patsy with a smile.

"I'm so proud of you—resisting all that junk food, Patsy! That must make you feel terrific!"

"I feel awful, Lori." Patsy heaved a great sigh and looked up at the ceiling.

"Hey! What's wrong?"

"Oh, Lori," Patsy said. "Losing the fat didn't make me happy. It just made me see how the world works—and it's awful, Lori."

Patsy's elfin face looked almost comical with its sad expression. A face like Patsy's, with its dimples and curls and dancing hazel eyes, was made for smiling, not for pouting.

"Come on," Lori chided, poking her friend in the arm. "Tell me you haven't been getting better treatment."

"Oh, I have— Everyone's been nicer to me."

"So why aren't you happy?"

"Well— It's great to be thin and all, but things still haven't changed for me with guys. Not one boy has asked me out yet. Maybe I'm just not, you know—pretty."

"Patsy Donovan, are you out of your mind?" Lori cried. "Listen to me. You're *gorgeous*! You're just so used to feeling fat that you don't know how to feel good about yourself."

"Yeah, sure. Miss Gorgeous—that's me—"

"Patsy. You just gave me a wild, but wonderful, idea." There was a giggle in Lori's voice now. "Why don't *you* enter the Miss Merivale Mall contest! You'd make the finals—I'd bet money on it! Would that convince you about your looks?"

"Me? Enter a beauty contest!? Not in a million years!" Patsy cried.

"The winner gets a two-thousand-dollar scholarship toward any college she gets accepted to—"

"A two-thousand-dollar scholarship! Miss Merivale Mall, huh?" Patsy put her hands on her slender hips and flashed a mile-wide grin. "Oh, why not? I've lost all those pounds, so what else do I have to lose? Where do I sign up?"

CHAPTER THREE

"Danielle Sharp." There was her name on the finalists' list posted on the board outside the mall's executive offices, just as she knew it would be. Right after Marcy Ryder and just before Ashley Shepard.

So much for the first hurdle. Danielle couldn't help breaking into a self-satisfied smile.

Not that she was surprised to see her name— between her own smashing good looks and the "heart-and-soul-of-Merivale" idea Lori had given her for the essay, there was no way they could have excluded her.

But Danielle's smile faded when she noticed Teresa Woods's name at the bottom of the list. She had been secretly hoping Teresa wouldn't make the finals at all. That would have *really* cut her friend's ego down to size.

Oh, well, things would just have to take their

natural course. In due time one of them would be wearing the crown, and the other would have to eat her words. "And I'm not going to eat mine," Danielle promised herself.

Danielle's eyes moved up the list, taking in the names of the other finalists. Most were girls she knew from school or around the mall. All the pretty girls at Atwood seemed to hang out together. No surprises there.

But one name made her gasp. Danielle had to look twice to see if she was reading it correctly.

"Patsy Donovan?" she gasped, her hand flying to her mouth to stifle her out-and-out shock. What was a tubette like Patsy Donovan doing in a beauty contest? And more amazing, *what was she doing in the finals?*

Danielle had to giggle. Somebody in the executive offices had apparently made a giant mistake. How else could poor deluded Miss Chubby Cheeks try out for Miss Merivale Mall?

"Fat" must be in these days, Danielle thought with a shrug.

"Oh, hi, Danielle." Spinning around, Danielle found herself staring into a pair of hazel eyes that looked familiar—*could it be?*

"I'm Patsy. Lori's friend, remember?" Danielle's eyes widened as she took in the new, improved Patsy. The big blob that used to be her face had thinned out and she was actually sort of pretty—in a wholesome way, of course.

"Oh, hi," Danielle muttered coolly, annoyed by this new circumstance. Danielle didn't like surprises; she liked being on top of everything. With a weak smile, she turned away. Only social-worker types, like her cousin Lori, even talked to Patsy Donovan. What a drag! Sharing the stage with a nonentity like Patsy Donovan brought the whole contest down for Danielle.

Just then the door of the executive offices opened, and Teresa Woods burst out like a shower of gold glitter. Her brown eyes were shining, and the expression on her face was one of total enthusiasm. At her elbow was Mr. Merivale Mall himself, the chief executive officer of the mall, Donald Ackers.

Leaning in to listen to Teresa, the tall, handsome executive seemed totally oblivious of the others gathered around the bulletin board.

"Thanks so-o much for the pointers." Teresa was gushing as she clutched a small booklet in her hands.

"Anytime, Miss Woods," was the executive's reply. "And if you need more information, just ask for me. I'm here to assist you, and I wish you all the luck in the world."

Looking up, Ackers finally saw the other contestants milling around outside the room.

"Ladies, congratulations," he said, throwing them a cursory nod before he fixed his eyes on Teresa's pretty brown ones again. "Please say hello to your father for me, dear."

"Oh, I will, Don." Teresa smiled and shook the executive's hand warmly. Then spinning around with a triumphant smile, she brushed past Danielle as if she didn't even know her.

It was as if a chilly wind swept over Danielle. But as Teresa breezed past, Danielle forced herself to look nonchalant and unconcerned.

Part of her wanted to yell out, "Come on. Let's forget all this stupid stuff." But another part of her was infuriated.

"Ladies, my assistant, Ms. Pierson, will give you all a set of the competition guidelines in just a second," Ackers announced after he watched Teresa walk toward the elevator. Then he disappeared into his offices without so much as a second glance at Danielle.

"Gee. It's a little scary, isn't it?" Patsy Donovan tried to smile at Danielle—the only person in the finals that she knew.

Danielle threw her a vague look, as if Patsy were speaking a foreign language. She didn't want to encourage this nonentity in any way.

The door opened just then. "Girls, I have your guidelines ready," said an older woman, whom Danielle took for Ackers's assistant. "On behalf of Mr. Ackers and the managing board of the mall, good luck." With that, she handed each girl the same booklet Teresa had been clutching moments before.

"Miss Merivale Mall Competition—Guidelines." The booklet was almost as long as the Constitution of the United States. It outlined all the competitions. There was a talent competition, a swimsuit competition, an evening gown competition, and an unrehearsed onstage interview, in which the contestant would be asked to answer two mystery questions.

Reading it, Danielle's heart began to pound. What could she possibly do for the talent competition? She didn't sing. Not really. And she didn't play the cello or anything. The only thing she really excelled at was math—nothing she could do with that. As for the interview—

Danielle gripped the edge of the desk tightly. *Calm down!* she ordered herself. It was ridiculous to feel so panicky. After all, with her looks, who needed talent? Besides, she couldn't afford to waste time worrying—she had important shopping to do.

Folding the booklet and stuffing it into her handbag, Danielle hurried off, trying to soothe her fears. She'd go to Facades and pick up a swimsuit. Just being in her favorite boutique, surrounded by glorious clothes, would help her calm down and think.

Stepping off the elevator and making her way to Facades, Danielle slowly regained her confidence. The swimsuit competition was going to be easy. Danielle was a knockout in a swimsuit.

Danielle pictured herself strutting proudly along the runway in a swimsuit and high heels. She'd just have to get a suit that was really fantastic. Maybe a white suit cut low to show off her back—

"Hi," Heather called and sauntered over to meet Danielle when she saw her walk into Facades. "Not that you care, but you just missed Teresa," she added.

"I just saw her," said Danielle offhandedly.

"I know. I heard all about it."

"Oh?" Danielle raised her eyebrow.

"She said you totally ignored her."

"She said *what*?" Danielle couldn't believe what she was hearing.

"She said you looked straight at her and didn't even say hello."

"She looked at *me* and didn't say hello," Danielle said emphatically.

"Well, according to her, you were jealous because she was talking to Ackers. You really shouldn't be, you know. He's an old family friend of the Woods."

"That's ridiculous. Why should I be jealous of her just because she was talking to Ackers?"

"Well, I think you're both being stupid." Heather turned away and began looking through a bunch of beach cover-ups. "My dad is meeting me in the Caribbean on winter break so I can meet his new wife."

Danielle found the swimsuits that Facades sold year-round. "Why don't they have anything in white?" she muttered. Then she lowered her voice and said conspiratorially, "Don't you think Teresa is being dumb? Can you picture her entering a swimsuit competition with those skinny legs of hers?"

"You're asking the wrong person," replied Heather in a sing-song voice. "I refuse to get caught between two giant egos like yours and Teresa's."

"I'm not saying it because of ego, Heather. It just happens to be a fact. Teresa has skinny legs."

Heather picked up and then discarded a beaded pink bikini. "Maybe, but her coach has a plan for that. She's got a whole set of special exercises just for her legs. She can't even go to the movies with me tonight—she's got to learn a whole Nautilus routine—"

Danielle froze. "Coach? What coach?"

"Her beauty contest coach. Didn't you know

that her parents hired this lady who was Miss Pennsylvania or something? Teresa's going to meet with her every day until the contest. The whole rest of her life is on hold, you know."

A coach? This contest was getting to be serious business. A coach must be costing the Woods a fortune, but then, they could afford it. Teresa would be getting professional guidance all along the way.

The panic started slowly, moving from Danielle's chest out through the rest of her body. Soon, she was hardly able to breathe, and her hands were shaking. *What if Teresa wins the contest? How horrible.*

Frantically grabbing swimsuits, Danielle rejected one after another. There wasn't one good suit on the whole rack. The best one was plain navy blue, and it was ugly.

With a snort of disdain, Danielle put the suit back on the rack. No way was she going to settle for a suit that wasn't perfect.

The same awful thought kept repeating over and over in her mind. It didn't matter what kind of suit she bought. No matter what she did, or how hard she tried, Teresa Woods was going to *buy* herself the title of Miss Merivale Mall!

CHAPTER FOUR

"Fail chemistry?" Lori Randall narrowed her bright blue eyes and looked past Ann Larson to a wincing Patsy Donovan. Behind the three friends, cafeteria trays rattled and dishes clattered as students made their way down the food line. "Patsy Donovan, how are you going to get into nursing school if you fail chemistry?"

"Beats me," Patsy moaned dolefully.

"Can't Irving help you?" Ann suggested. Irving Zalaznick, fellow Merivale High junior and scientific wizard extraordinaire, was Patsy's lab partner. Lucky for Patsy too. They were such a good team that their lab projects always got A's.

Irving always helped Patsy study, and once he'd even helped her get revenge on Heather Barron and Teresa Woods for setting her up on a phony date with someone who didn't want to go out with her. Irving had found a formula to turn hair kelly green, and she managed to sneak it into Heather and Teresa's shampoo—with incredible results.

Irving Zalaznick—fellow reject, thought Patsy as she picked at her sandwich. Irving was short and he always wore wrinkled shirts. His trousers were either too long or too baggy or both.

Guys shunned him because he wasn't an athlete. And most girls thought he was a nerd, just because he wore glasses and liked science.

"Patsy? Earth to Patsy—" Lori had to smile at the dazed look on her friend's face. "We *were* talking about chemistry? You *did* say, you might *flunk*, didn't you?"

"Oh, Lori, you don't understand! Failing chemistry is only the beginning! I still have the whole Miss Merivale Mall contest to think about. I mean, can you picture *me* up on a stage competing with girls like your cousin Danielle and Teresa Woods? And what am I going to do for my talent? And where am I ever going to find the right evening gown?"

"Slow down, Patsy!" Lori suggested. "Just take things one at a time."

"Lori's right," advised Ann, reaching for a carton of apple juice. She ran a finger through her lustrous brown hair, her soft gray eyes riveted on her formerly pudgy pal. "And I can help you out with a biggie right away. I know exactly what you should do for your talent."

"You do? What?" Patsy sounded as if she were being rescued from drowning.

"Your aerobic routine, silly! You've really got it down, and you do it great!" Under Ann's guidance Patsy had been working on an aerobic dance routine ever since she first started losing weight.

"It's true, Patsy!" Lori agreed. "Every time I see you do that routine, it makes me want to stand up and cheer."

"Well," murmured Patsy, "I suppose I could do it for the talent section, if I put in some harder moves—"

"As for the gown—well, I don't know if you'd be interested, but I do want to work on a formal gown—"

"Lori, if you're offering to make my gown for me, the answer is a definite *yes*!" Patsy cried.

"See? There are two problems solved, and we just got started." Ann laughed.

"As for the swimsuit, you'll just have to go shopping!" said Lori.

"Ergh, the very word makes my skin crawl," Patsy moaned. "Every time I ever went shopping for a bathing suit, I broke out all over in big blotches. No kidding!"

"That's because you were overweight, Patsy," Lori said. "Wait'll you see yourself in a size six or seven."

"Well, that's all fantastic, but"—Patsy shifted uncomfortably in her chair—"no matter how good I supposedly look, I'm still invisible as far as boys are concerned. Every Saturday night it's me alone at home, watching TV. Ugh." Patsy flung her head down on her arms and sighed dramatically.

"Patsy, how can you be depressed?" Ann demanded. "You're perfect now. You're thin! You're everything you've always wanted to be."

Patsy lifted her head up far enough so only her chin was on her arms. She peered straight ahead and heaved another sigh. "It is what I've always wanted. I am thin. I am a whole new person. But every boy in the world still ignores me." And her head flopped back down again.

"It's tough being *lonely*." Lori reached across the table and touched her friend gently on the arm.

Patsy looked up and attempted to smile.

"Yeah, lonely—that's me. I mean, what good is being a finalist if I can't even get a date! No wonder I can't concentrate on chemistry! My future as a lonely spinster keeps haunting me."

"Patsy, please," moaned Ann.

Patsy looked positively peeved. "Well, how

would you feel if the only male who ever wanted to kiss you was your dog?"

"May I make a suggestion?" asked Lori gently.

"Sure, go ahead."

"I know you've worked hard to lose that weight, but maybe you're not used to the new you. Maybe you're still trying to hide."

Patsy looked interested. "What do you mean?" she asked.

"I know what Lori means. Your clothes, for instance. They could use a little improvement," Ann threw in. "That jumper looked great on your mom, but it's just too big for you."

"It does kind of hide your shape, Patsy," Lori agreed.

"Hmmm." Patsy's face took on a thoughtful expression. When she had first lost weight, she took every hand-me-down she could just to have something to wear.

"You need a few new things that *you* picked out, things that really fit." Ann went on. "I promise you, a couple of pairs of size seven jeans and you'll have the guys running after you in hordes."

"Maybe when you go shopping for your swimsuit, you can get some other stuff—stuff that really fits."

"Well, I do have some savings," Patsy said. "While I was dieting I put all my cheesecake

money in a cheesecake box under my bed—and
as long as I'm going shopping *anyway*. . ."

"Fantastic! You'll do the aerobic routine for
your talent. I'll make you a gown. Irv'll help
you with chemistry. You'll get a new wardrobe
and look fantastic. See, all your problems are
solved!" Lori smiled and reached across the table to squeeze Patsy's arm.

"Well, since you put it that way," said Patsy,
"anybody want to help me do some shopping
after work?"

"Me! Me! Me!" Lori cried. Shopping was a
blast for Lori. She didn't allow herself to indulge in it very often—not even window-shopping.
But by going with Patsy, she could see what
was new in the stores and help a friend at the
same time.

"Just promise me one thing, Patsy," said Ann.
"When you see yourself in the mirror, don't get
a swelled head."

Danielle had thought it over all the way home.
Riding along the streets of Merivale in her white
BMW, everything had become a lot clearer. If
Teresa Woods hired a coach to help her win the
contest, Danielle had better hire one too.

That night when her father walked through
the door, she was ready for him. "Hi, Daddy!"
she called out perkily.

"Hi, Danielle," he replied, loosening the knot of his tie and tiredly running a hand through his thick, dark hair. "Is your mother home?"

"Not yet. She's out shopping, but she said she'd be back before supper."

"I suppose we're eating late then, as usual." Her father sounded irritated. "Well, I'm going upstairs to lie down."

"Daddy? Can I talk to you about something?" Danielle's heart was thundering in her chest. "Did you know I made the finals in the Miss Merivale Mall contest?" she asked before he could get a word in.

"No, I didn't, Princess. But that's great." Danielle could tell her father was genuinely pleased.

"And Daddy"—this was the hard part—"I was thinking, you know, a lot of girls in the competition are hiring coaches to help them, and I thought maybe I should get a coach too—"

Suddenly the light faded from Mike Sharp's eyes.

"Oh, really?" he said icily. "And how much do these 'coaches' cost, Danielle?"

Gulping hard, Danielle forced her mouth into a bright smile. "I don't know—maybe a thousand dollars or something—but it's worth it, Daddy. They help you all the way through."

"Danielle, you do realize that I'm already

spending a mint for riding lessons, a private school, a health club, and an expensive car. And that's not counting your monthly allowance. The coach is out of the question."

Getting her father to change his mind about anything was almost impossible, Danielle knew. She could feel herself breaking into a fine sweat around her hairline. "But, Daddy, maybe I could skip riding lessons—"

The muscles around Danielle's father's jaw were clenched now. "The answer is no, Danielle. And I don't want you to ask me about this again, do you understand?"

"Yes, Dad," Danielle answered meekly. Her father wasn't in the mood for an argument, and she wasn't about to give him one.

"Thank you." With that, he strode up the steps to his bedroom and Danielle could hear the door close with a definite click. Her father obviously was having a bad day.

Danielle sunk into the beige leather sofa in the living room and tried to collect her thoughts. There had to be a way to get a coach for the contest. A way her father didn't have to know about it. She'd just have to get the money from someone else. . . .

*   *   *

Serena Sharp was standing beside the kitchen desk, looking over the weekly menu from Premier Caterers when Danielle found her an hour later.

"Oh, hi, Mom!"

"Hello, darling," her mother answered distractedly. "Should we have veal or filet of sole tomorrow?"

Choosing dishes was as close as Mrs. Sharp ever got to cooking. But even making those choices seemed to weigh on her.

"I like veal."

"Yes, but we had it last week."

"Then order the sole."

"But sole is so fishy."

"How about steak?"

"I'm ordering shrimp, and that's that."

"Guess what, Mom? I have some good news."

"Really, dear? What is it?" her mother asked, marking the menu.

"I made the finals in the Miss Merivale Mall contest."

Mrs. Sharp dropped her pencil and looked up at Danielle. Dismay flashed across her perfectly made-up eyes. "Danielle, is this a joke? I never know when you're joking."

"It's not a joke. There's a Miss Merivale Mall contest, and I got into the finals. There are only ten finalists from the whole town."

A stunned look came over her mother's face. "Poor Danielle. You don't really think— I mean, beauty contests are so—tasteless. I don't think you should get involved in anything like that, honey."

Oh, why did talking to her mother always make her feel so awful! "I'm already in it, Mom. So is Teresa—"

"The Woods are allowing it? I'm surprised."

"They're not just 'allowing' it, Mom, they *want* Teresa to win! They hired a coach for her and everything."

"Isn't that silly— Is your father home?"

"He's upstairs. But, Mother, hiring a coach isn't *really* ridiculous. It might help Teresa become Miss Merivale Mall!"

Moving out of the kitchen into the skylit living room, Mrs. Sharp shot her daughter a look of withering condescension. "If you're asking whether Daddy and I will hire a coach for *you*, the answer is absolutely not. If I were you, I would drop out immediately."

"But I can't!" Danielle cried. "Everybody would say I dropped out because I was scared!"

"Well, I can't help what people think. We are not going to hire a coach, I'm sorry. I don't want to hear any more about it. By the way, there's food in the refrigerator."

Thanks a lot, Mother! So much for getting a

coach to help her out. Teresa would win the contest now and lord it over Danielle for years—that snob.

Danielle tried to hold it back, but a tear sneaked down her cheek. Then another. *"Why?"* she asked out loud, as if Teresa were there with her. *Why can't we just be friends again, like we used to be?*

CHAPTER FIVE

When Patsy Donovan walked into Merivale High wearing a pair of size seven jeans and a light coat of mascara on her thick reddish brown lashes, the results were amazing.

In homeroom Bill Evans—sprained ankle and all—stood up when Patsy crossed in front of him to get to her seat. Bill's injury had been big news around Merivale High. Bill Evans was the fullback for the Merivale Vikings and one of the most popular guys in school.

"Patsy, wow—I mean, hi," he gulped, pulling himself up to his feet. He leaned on the chair in front of him with a strong, slender arm.

"Oh, hi," replied a startled Patsy. Although they'd known each other for three years, it was the first time Bill had ever said "hello" to her. Occasionally, he nodded—but not often.

But *now*, there he was, standing and looking at her as if he'd never seen her before. Patsy started feeling tingly all over as she desperately tried to think of something cool to say. Bill's good looks were positively intimidating. He had short blond hair, perfectly tousled, and a year-round tan. And not only was he a football hero, he was an actor too. He usually starred in the spring play.

Patsy shifted her books from one hip to the other. She shot him a look from the corner of her eyes. It felt so strange—getting attention from a guy who, until just now, had ignored her completely. Patsy looked down at her books, then broke out in a shy grin. "Excuse me, Bill. Could I get by, please?"

"Oh, of course!" She seemed to have caught him off guard. "Congratulations on the contest, Patsy." He took a quick look around and lowered his voice. "I get rid of this thing tomorrow." He pointed to his Ace bandage.

"Oh?" Patsy wasn't sure what to say next. But she didn't have to worry about it, because Bill wasn't finished yet.

"Want to go to the movies Wednesday night?" He tossed it out matter-of-factly, as if it was every day that they went out together.

Bill Evans was asking her out! Patsy sputtered her reply. "Um—sure! I'd love to. I just need to make sure I can get off work first."

Patsy was not about to let a little thing like a job stand in her way at a moment like this, but she needed an excuse, just in case she couldn't handle it at the last moment.

"Well, I know you're busy with the finals and all, but let me know, okay?" Bill sat down and threw her a grin and a wink, then started leafing through one of his notebooks.

When the morning bell rang, Patsy ducked down the hall to her first-period Spanish class. Ann and Lori were on the opposite side of the building and she wouldn't see them till lunch, but wait till they heard—Bill Evans had asked her out!

In the hallway a couple of kids said "Hi," but most ignored Patsy as usual. The old anonymity felt good. When she had been talking to Bill, she almost felt as if she were onstage. It felt terrific, but it had really thrown her too. She must have seemed dumb standing there saying, "Oh." But, then—she couldn't have been too dumb, because Bill had still asked her out.

"Where's Mr. Rodriguez?" Patsy asked a group of kids who were standing in the front of the room.

Amanda George filled her in. "In the audiovisual room. We're seeing a film today. But they're having trouble with the projector."

Hmmm. Patsy took her seat. But instead of reaching for her Spanish book, she took out her copy of *Advanced Chemistry Today.* Having a few extra minutes to go over her lab assignment would definitely be good. She could use all the extra time she could get.

The only trouble was, how could she think about ions and hydrogen when her head was swimming and her heart was beating wildly in her chest? She was thin, and pretty, and Bill Evans liked her!

He had been so sincere about it too—as if he had been secretly interested in her all along. But he sure never let on—guys were a mystery.

"Psst! Patsy, do you have an extra pen?"

Patsy turned in her seat to see Steve Kirkwood smiling at her. Steve Kirkwood was the only guy at Merivale High who was just possibly cuter than Bill Evans. Steve was just over six feet, and his eyes were a magnetic blue— made even bluer by the contrast with his dark, curly hair.

"An extra pen?" Patsy fumbled through her new bag. "Sorry, Steve. I don't."

"That's okay." In the time he took to say it, Steve had gotten up from his seat and moved to the one next to her. "That's fantastic about the

Miss Merivale Mall contest." She nodded shyly. "What are you reading?" He leaned across the aisle and she caught a whiff of his after-shave. She had always wondered what it was, it smelled so good.

"This! Oh, uh—chemistry," she stammered, burying her nose in the book. *What in the world is happening?*

She waited for him to move back to his seat, but Steve didn't seem in any hurry. Flustered, Patsy tried to read.

"Electromagnetic ions . . . subatomic particles . . . quasars . . . quarks . . . hydrogen . . . nitrogen . . ." The words were a blur.

Steve was still leaning in close. "Ah, yes— electromagnetic ions—"

What is he talking about? Patsy looked up and smiled. "Excuse me?" she asked. *Oh, why is talking to guys so hard?*

"Good stuff there." He pointed to her book. "I never realized you were so brainy. But even a genius needs time off. How would you like to go out with me sometime soon?"

Unless there was something radically wrong with her hearing, Steve Kirkwood, junior class president, track star, and world-class hunk had just asked her out too! *Who said lightning doesn't strike twice in the same place?*

* * *

During lunch Patsy tried to remain calm and poised and open her tuna sandwich at the same time. But her fingers were jumping with excitement, just like her heart.

"What are you two so happy about?" she whispered to Lori and Ann, who were sitting across the table from her, beaming.

"Well, come on, Pats! You've got to admit having *two* guys ask you out in one day is really something to shout about!" replied Lori.

"I think it's because of the Miss Merivale Mall contest. Seeing my picture in the paper must have done something to them. But I don't know how to handle this! What should I do?"

"Go with the flow." Ann laughed. "The fickle finger of fate is obviously pointed straight at you."

"Yeah, enjoy it!" Lori added.

"Enjoy it? It's too overwhelming to enjoy!"

"Can you beat that?" Ann said with a laugh. "Even when she gets what she wants, she's not happy!"

"Yeah, cheer up, Patsy," Lori agreed. "Things could be a lot worse, after all."

"But what am I going to do?" moaned Patsy. "Do you realize that the last time I was out on a real date was in junior high? I went bowling with Chuckie Wootzer. Hot time."

The three girls giggled together. Patsy's mood

was brightening in spite of her best efforts to remain glum.

"Besides, how can I ever chose between two guys like Bill Evans and Steve Kirkwood? I can't go out with *both* of them!" Patsy buried her face in her hands, then slowly drew her fingers aside and asked mischievously, "Can I?"

"Oh, it has been known to happen one or two times—" Lori said teasingly.

"Oh, Lori, I'm in *awe* of guys like them. They're so good-looking, so popular—I mean, this is totally surreal! I'm talking dreamland. Fantasy time. This can't be happening to me—"

"Guess it's time your dreams came true," said Lori.

Patsy sighed. "Sounds good, Lori, if I don't blow it. It's a good thing I'm failing chemistry, and that I have to compete in the contest. It'll give me something else to think about besides the butterflies in my stomach!"

In the chem lab Irving Zalaznick was hunched over his desk, scribbling into his spiral notebook and looking up every few minutes to check the Bunsen burner.

Patsy poked absently at the concoction in the beaker with a metal instrument. The butterflies in her stomach were moving in high gear, just like the rainbow-colored liquid in the beaker.

Bill Evans, Steve Kirkwood, Miss Merivale Mall—around and around and around . . .

"Hey, Patsy! What are you doing?" cried Irving as the mixture in the beaker began to fizz. "We're not supposed to stir that stuff!"

Patsy grabbed the beaker and took it away from the burner. "Sorry, Irv. It's just—"

"It's okay. I guess you have a lot on your mind lately, with the contest and all." Everyone in school had noticed Patsy's new looks and her recent successes. It was impossible *not* to notice. "Must be great to be Miss Popularity. So how come you're not smiling?"

"Well, it is a little strange getting all this attention all of a sudden, you know? I mean, I keep asking myself what I did to deserve it, and I can't think of anything. In a way, I'm not sure I like it."

Irving nodded thoughtfully. "Maybe I'm not so bad off after all—" He smiled wryly, pushed his glasses back up on his nose, and reopened his notebook. "We'd better get to work, huh? We don't want you failing chem on top of all these other 'catastrophes.' "

By the end of the period Irving and Patsy—Irving, mostly—had come up with an absolute A-plus lab report. Patsy's outlook on life had improved tremendously in just forty-five minutes. Still, there was something missing for her.

Even though she wasn't completely bummed out, she wasn't completely *happy* either.

What was *wrong* with her, anyway? She was thin, she was popular, she had dates lined up with two of the best-looking boys in school— and it looked as if she might even pass chemistry. So why did she still feel that empty feeling inside?

CHAPTER SIX

The minute Atwood classes let out, Danielle raced to the parking lot, got into her BMW, and made tracks for the mall. The whole Miss Merivale Mall contest was getting completely out of hand, and it was time for her to take action.

What had started as a little fight with her pal, Teresa, had snowballed into World War Three, and Danielle had to make sure *she* had the best ammunition.

First on the agenda was a swimsuit. Danielle hurried into Paradise Isle. Unfortunately, the new swimsuits weren't on the racks yet. She'd have to select from a meager group—or worse, cruisewear.

Still, Danielle didn't need novelty. With her perfect legs and figure, topped off by her amazing red hair—well, no girl in Merivale could actually compete with her and win. When it came to the swimsuit competition, she was sure she'd blow the other girls right out of the water.

Half an hour later Danielle found a white suit with black piping that *almost* met her standards. She gave the other fifteen back to the sales woman and moved on to Facades.

Evening gowns. Getting the right gown was going to be a little more complicated. There was so much more to a gown. And Facades, as Danielle knew, had a limited supply. Not that any other store was even worth looking in.

The moment Danielle stepped into her favorite boutique, she sensed victory. And she was rewarded for there, on display, was the most exquisite formal dress she had ever seen. It was a strapless fuchsia gown with a boa wrap, and it was *perfect*!

Danielle found the gown in size seven and held it up to her. The bright color highlighted her hair, making it a crown of fire. No judge could resist her in this dress. And she had found it on the very first try!

Suddenly Danielle heard a familiar voice behind her. "Ugh. Too tight. Too tight under the arms. I'd never be able to accept the roses in this!" That voice could belong to only one girl— sure enough, Teresa Woods was in the store, too!

Frantically looking around for a hiding place, Danielle put the gown back and spied a rack of oversized coats a few feet away. She hunched over to make herself small, and ducked behind them before Teresa could see her.

"But I want to try the fuchsia gown! It's really fantastic, and it'll look great with my hair," Teresa was insisting.

Danielle could have kicked herself. *Why didn't I come here before I got the swimsuit?* Now Teresa was going to scoop up the one gown Danielle would have chosen for herself, and Danielle was going to be stuck with leftovers!

Through the coats, Danielle saw a woman who looked like a movie star talking to Teresa. The woman was dressed to perfection in a smart beige suit, and except for a few lines around her eyes, she still looked like the beauty contest winner she once was. Danielle knew in an instant that she was Teresa's coach.

"Sweetie, let me tell you a story," she was saying. "When I was crowned Miss Pennsylvania, I chose a pale pink dress with puffed sleeves. Judges tend to favor pink, if the shade is subtle— but you've got to be careful. Last year, in the Miss Universe competition, if you remember, Miss U.S.A. wore a bright gown. It was exactly that fuchsia shade. She came in fourth, even though everyone expected her to walk away with the title. When I spoke with the judges afterward, they all mentioned that dress. It was far too garish, and that one mistake cost her the crown."

Teresa was sobered. "Oh—" she murmured.

"Don't worry, Teresa. We're *not* going to let that happen to you." The coach put a reassuring arm around Teresa's slender shoulders.

"Barbi, I don't know what I'd do without you," gushed a grateful Teresa. "I'd just be lost!"

Like I am! thought Danielle, her heart sinking as she craned her neck through the coats.

"May I help you?" The saleswoman's voice sounded as loud as a bomb to Danielle.

"No thank you," whispered Danielle hoarsely, "I'm just looking . . . " *Please—go away!*

"Well, if you need any help . . ." Looking at Danielle with a puzzled expression, the saleswoman backed away, and Danielle returned to her hiding place.

"Well, here are the two best," the coach told Teresa, scooping up a pale pink and a lavender gown. "The others are inappropriate, I'm afraid, lovely as they are. But I think one of these will do very well."

Teresa sighed. "You're really a big help!"

"Well, that's what I'm here for!" Barbi, the coach, replied cheerfully.

Teresa and her coach disappeared into the fitting room, and Danielle came out of her hiding place to look at the rejected gowns. They were exquisite. But the coach had called them inappropriate— How could Danielle trust her own taste anymore? And if she couldn't trust herself, who could she trust?

"Oh, yes. Yes! This is it!" Barbi's voice was definite.

Danielle rushed back to her hiding place and craned her neck to look at Teresa. What she saw gave her a giant-sized headache. Teresa Woods was an absolute vision in a soft pink satin gown.

"It's perfect," Barbi announced, "just perfect. It's youthful, but sophisticated—elegant, and above all, feminine. *This* is the gown the judges will be looking for—and *you'll* be wearing it."

Danielle gazed at her friend in wonder. Teresa had only had a coach for a day or two, and already she was looking better than she had ever looked in her life! If she looked this good now, what was she going to look like by the time the contest came around?

Teresa twirled happily in front of the mirror, her big brown eyes sparkling with delight as she took herself in. "Gosh," she uttered breathlessly. "I do look pretty good!"

"You look fabulous! Enjoy it, Teresa, because

you're looking at the first ever Miss Merivale
Mall. And I promise you, this is only the beginning. Between your beauty and your talent
as a pianist, you truly have the potential to go
on to be Miss America, or even Miss Universe. I
mean it. The last two girls I coached made it to
the top, and you can too." The coach was so
confident and assuring to Teresa that Danielle
wanted to scream.

"It is gorgeous. But shouldn't I try on the
lavender too, just for comparison?" asked the
beaming Teresa, without tearing her eyes away
from her own lovely image.

"Hmmm—I suppose you should. After you
win the crown you'll need a few extra evening
gowns for the appearances you'll have to make.
Besides, why leave a great dress behind for
another contestant to find? Go ahead and try it
on, and after that we can work on your poise
and diction."

Sighing happily, Teresa lifted the skirt of her
long dress and made her way back to the dressing room with a radiant smile on her lips.

Watching her go, Danielle sank into the coats
and gritted her teeth in frustration. If Teresa
Woods showed up wearing that "elegant, sophisticated, yet feminine" gown, the judges
would fall down at her feet. She'd walk away
with the title for sure.

Because let's face it, Danielle thought, *in the evening gown competition it's the gown, not the girl, that wins or loses.*

Grabbing a purple oversized coat from the rack in front of her to avert suspicion, Danielle slipped into the dressing area as quietly as she could. She'd just have to take charge of the situation. She didn't have a coach to help her, so she had to do something to help herself—quick!

Inside one of the changing rooms, she could hear Teresa humming. The pink evening dress was slung over the door to the room.

Danielle reached up and pulled the gown down in an instant. Deftly she hid it under the oversized coat on her arm. Flushed with a heady sense of excitement, she rushed to the cashier at the other end of the store. She knew that she had only seconds to get out of the store.

"Oh, hello, Miss Sharp. Will that be cash or charge?" To Danielle it sounded as if the cashier was yelling at the top of her lungs.

"Please, wrap this up right away," she murmured to the waiting cashier.

"That will be two hundred forty-seven dollars," the cashier noted, snipping the tag off the dress. "Will this be cash or charge?"

Danielle's heart caught in her throat, but she stammered out, "Charge." Victory was going to be costly, but then, defeat would be too unbearably awful for words.

"Please hurry," she urged impatiently. "I have a fur fitting upstairs."

It was only a little lie. Maybe it would make the salesgirl work more quickly. The last thing she wanted was for Teresa to catch her red-handed—or should she say, pink-handed.

When the clerk finally handed her the package, Danielle walked out of the store with a spring in her step. Mission accomplished!

"Thanks a billion, Teresa dear," Danielle said to herself as she raced down the escalator steps two at a time. The pink satin evening dress was sure to be a perfect fit. After all, she and Teresa wore the exact same size.

All the way home, Danielle couldn't help smiling wickedly at the thought of Teresa searching for the absent gown; imagining her face when she saw Danielle wearing it onstage. That would serve her right—the nerve of Teresa—putting their friendship on the line over a stupid beauty contest!

Safe in her room, Danielle pulled the dress out of a cloud of tissue paper and held it up to herself as she walked to the mirror. But when she tripped on the skirt, a horrible feeling began to creep over her. Taking a look at the tag, her worst fears were confirmed. *Size fourteen!*

Just then, as if on cue, the phone rang. Danielle had a sickening feeling that she knew who it was, and she was right.

"Oh, hi, Danielle," Teresa's voice purred on the other end of the line. "I was just wondering how you like your new evening gown. By the way, how does it fit? It must look great with that purple coat you had on your arm."

Before Danielle could scream a word in reply, the phone went dead in her hands.

That little rat! She had known all along that Danielle was in the store and had planted that gargantuan dress as a decoy! Talk about sneaky tricks!

Shaking with fury, Danielle picked up the dress in her fists. If only she could afford to rip it to shreds . . . but she'd have to return it to get her money back.

"Oh, you little witch!" she spat out. "You want to play dirty? Well, just remember, you asked for it. . . ."

CHAPTER SEVEN

Patsy was spraying a cloud of cologne around her shoulders when the doorbell rang. Her mother had given her the bottle of Spring Awakening for her birthday and she'd been waiting for just the right occasion to wear it. But never in her wildest dreams did she imagine it would be for a date with Bill Evans.

"Mom, I'll get it!" she called, racing downstairs to open the front door.

"Hi, Patsy." There was Bill, all right. With his blond hair, piercing blue eyes, and navy crew sweater, Bill looked as if he had just stepped off the pages of a magazine.

But it was the dimple in his chin, and the way he cocked his head when he said hello that knocked the breath right out of Patsy. "Bill—uh, you're here."

Come on, Donovan, you can do better than that! the little voice inside her was saying.

"All ready?" he murmured, stepping inside.

Was it her imagination or was he sneaking a peek at himself in the hall mirror?

Patsy couldn't help taking a quick look at herself too. The girl looking back at her was terrific looking. It made Patsy feel a little weird, as if the old Patsy were lost somewhere, hidden just out of sight.

"I guess I'm about ready," she said, turning to him, and hoping she wouldn't wobble on her new heels.

"Mom, I'm going," Patsy called to the kitchen.

"Hold on, honey, let me say good-bye first." Mrs. Donovan walked into the living room, a dish towel in her hand. She was a portly woman with the same lively hazel eyes as her daughter. Patsy could tell from the look on her face when she saw Bill that her mother was impressed.

"Oh, hello," Mrs. Donovan sputtered, hiding the dish towel behind her back. "You must be Patsy's friend."

"Mom, this is Bill Evans," Patsy said.

"Well, hello, Bill." Mrs. Donovan was smiling so broadly that Patsy wanted to sink into the nylon carpeting. But Bill didn't seem embarrassed in the least.

"Well, Patsy, we'd better be going. Nice meeting you, Mrs. Donovan," he said with a little wave.

"Have a good time, kids," Patsy's mother called after them.

"And don't worry, Mrs. Donovan, I'll get her home safe and sound." And with that, they walked outside and Bill opened the car door for her.

It was all so thrilling! The pride on her mother's face, the way Bill was so polite, the way he said "All ready?" It was such a great start— now she had to hope she wouldn't blow it.

Bill probably went out all the time. Last year he and a cheerleader were going steady, but this year he seemed to be playing the field. *Picture me in the same league as a cheerleader*, Patsy thought.

When she slid nervously over the seat of Bill's Mustang, she wondered for a moment if she was wearing too much perfume.

"So. Did you have a particular movie in mind?" she asked, hating herself for the tremor in her voice. "I hear there were a few good ones around."

"I figured we'd see *Hotel Warriors*."

"Oh? *Hotel Warriors*?" Patsy nodded agreeably. "Never heard of it. What's it about?"

"It's a kung fu movie. Supposed to be really

great too." Bill glanced into the rearview mirror and ran a hand over his wheat blond hair, tousling it carefully. "You'll like it. I promise."

"Oh." Patsy tried to hide her disappointment. Tilting her head to one side while Bill concentrated on driving, Patsy bit her lip and wondered if all guys decided on the movie before they picked the girl up. She thought people consulted about things like that. But then, she reminded herself, she really didn't have enough experience to know how it worked.

"I just saw *Cruise Ship Warriors*. It was great," Bill said.

"Really?" Patsy replied. "I missed that one."

"Truly great movie. Two guys are on a cruise ship going to a karate championship in the Bahamas when all of a sudden this group of international terrorists comes on board. Really fantastic. You know, I'm a brown belt—"

"Really?" Patsy remembered reading in some teen magazine that a girl should show interest in her date to "draw him out." But Bill didn't seem to need any drawing out. He seemed more than willing to talk about himself.

"Yeah. I'll be a black belt next year. I figure I should be able to compete pretty soon. They tell me I've made the quickest progress of anybody they've ever seen. I have the strength and I'm agile. That means quick."

"I know."

"Of course, I may have to pull out of some of my karate training and football because I want to get into acting very seriously. With my looks and all, I figure I'm a natural. Wouldn't want to risk my face, know what I mean? Besides, acting's so easy. All I really have to do is get up on stage. Maybe it's the karate training but I just have a lot of presence, you know?"

"Really?" Talking to Bill was turning out to be a lot easier than Patsy imagined it would be. All she had to do was nod her head, and she came off like a great conversationalist.

Besides that, Patsy noticed that Bill had no trouble talking and driving and looking at himself in the rearview mirror, all at the same time.

"The way I figure it," he continued, pulling the car into the parking lot, "some people have it, and some people don't. I mean, I don't want to sound conceited or anything, but let's face it. There aren't a lot of guys like me around. Smart, natural athletic ability, good looks . . . What can I say? I'm a pretty lucky guy. Not that luck has anything to do with it. Well, maybe the looks— And here we are."

Bill pulled into a space and turned off the engine. The two of them got out of the car and walked up to the Sixplex Movie Theater. In the lobby Patsy noticed Bill secretly observing himself in a copper-toned mirror. Was he looking for something wrong? If he was, he was wasting his time. Every part of Bill Evans looked perfect.

Don't be judgmental, Patsy warned herself. *After all, anybody as good-looking as he would want to look at himself!*

By the time *Hotel Warriors* let out, Patsy couldn't lie to herself one more minute. Bill Evans was an egomaniac. He seemed to carry an invisible mirror in front of his face at all times.

"You know, the movie was okay. But the lead was weak. . . ."

Patsy politely stifled her yawns on the ride home. The entire evening had come and gone without Bill showing even a dot of interest in her. He never even asked her what she thought of the movie—which was probably just as well.

"Soooo!" Lori's blue eyes were twinkling mischievously as she leaned on Patsy's arm in the hall the next day. "How was it?"

Patsy didn't say a word, but the way she rolled her eyes up and shook her head told Lori everything. "Know what I kept asking myself all night? How can anybody who looks that good be that boring?"

"No good, huh?" Lori murmured sympathetically.

"And on top of that, McFarlane announced a review test next week in chemistry! Oh, Lori, I'm definitely going to flunk. I just know it. Then it's good-bye scholarship, good-bye nursing school, good-bye future!"

"But, Pats, can't you study for it? You have a week."

"Forget it, Lori. I need a little longer than a week to catch up in chemistry. A year would be more like it."

"Aw, come on now—you can't be *that* far behind."

"I'm *way* behind. Lately, when McFarlane lectures I feel like I'm listening to a Martian. He keeps talking about oxyclothene and polymorphotanes, things like that."

"What are they?"

"Beats me!"

"Cheer up, Patsy. You'll just have to burn the midnight oil, but you can do it!" With that, Lori affectionately threw an arm around her friend's shoulder.

"I can?" said Patsy with a sigh. "Oh, I hope you're right, Lor. But let me remind you, you thought going out with Bill Evans was going to be a dream come true."

"Mmmm—" Lori bit her lip and frowned.

"Sorry about that. He *looked* good, but maybe you'll have a better time with Steve Kirkwood."

"Hmmm—Steve Kirkwood, that's right. I forgot about him. Oh, Lori! He's so cute, I can't stand it."

"You're pretty cute yourself, Donovan. In case you didn't notice."

"Sure, sure. Tell that to the Miss Merivale Mall judges."

The heels of Danielle Sharp's gray suede boots made a clicking sound as she walked down the almost empty halls of Atwood Academy. *Why is my life falling apart?* she moaned miserably to herself. The beauty pageant was a little more than a week away, and she was totally unprepared. Teresa was going to win the stupid title and then, boy, would Danielle look like a jerk.

"Hi, Danielle!" Wendy Carter's nauseatingly cheerful voice broke through Danielle's dark thoughts. "Did you see Teresa?"

Wendy evidently hadn't picked up on the fact that she and Teresa weren't exactly the best of friends these days. But then, Wendy had the sensitivity of a porcupine.

"No, where was she?" Danielle replied demurely.

"She was just showing us sketches of her new dress—the one she's going to wear in the evening gown competition. You should see it, Danielle. It's fantastic!"

"It is?"

"Truly spectacular. It's pink satin and it has—"

Danielle had to get out of there. Hearing about Teresa's fantastic gown was just too much. "Oh, *where* are my car keys?" she muttered distractedly.

"By the way, Danielle, what are *you* doing for *your* talent?" Wendy looked so bright and eager that Danielle wanted to scream.

Danielle crinkled up her nose, cutesy style, and giggled. "Oh, it's my little secret." Some secret. Even she didn't have a clue. "See you, Wendy. I've got to run!"

Waving to Wendy, Danielle made her way down the hall to the back exit as fast as she could. She had a lot of thinking to do, a lot of figuring out. After all, she was a great person, wasn't she? She *had* to have some kind of talent—besides shopping!

But what?

In third grade she had learned a few folk dances, but Ashley Shepard's ballet from *Swan Lake* would eclipse the Mexican hat dance any day.

Musical instrument? The only thing she knew how to play was the stereo.

Sighing at the thought of it all, Danielle headed for the exit when suddenly a swell of music from the music department stopped her in her tracks.

Someone was playing soft lush strains of classical music on the school's baby grand.

Through the door, the muted sound of the piano reached deep into Danielle. Every chord, every note of the glorious music seemed to express the precise way she was feeling.

Danielle stood and listened, tears glistening in her emerald eyes. All the tension she had been carrying inside melted away. Drinking the music in, Danielle felt herself relax for the first time all day.

Then the music stopped, and Teresa Woods poked her head out the door. That gorgeous piano playing belonged to Teresa, the rat!

"Why, hello, Danielle." Teresa's voice was like ice. "Waiting for the piano?"

"No, just wondering who was butchering Beethoven, or Bach, or whoever that was," Danielle said, watching her pretty ex-friend walk away.

But Teresa wasn't about to let Danielle have the last word. At the end of the hall, she turned and called out with a vicious little giggle, "It was Rachmaninoff, actually. Oh, by the way, Danielle, what are *you* doing for *your* talent?"

CHAPTER EIGHT

It hit Danielle on the way home. Tap dancing! When she was in junior high, she had taken lessons and learned a whole routine. Best, she had always looked so adorable in those little costumes! How could she have forgotten!

Danielle raced to her room and began rifling through her closet. Sure enough, in the back was her old canvas dance bag.

Unzipping the bag, Danielle smiled with relief. The black patent tap shoes still looked good; in fact, they looked almost new.

Danielle tried to get the shoes on. Unfortunately, they were about two sizes too small. She grabbed a pair of sharp scissors and began to cut holes out in them. She could always get a new pair at the mall.

When she was done, Danielle ran to her record collection and began flipping through looking for "Tea for Two." All those Saturday-morning lessons with Lori were finally going to pay off!

But when the song came on and Danielle listened to the familiar strains of the old soft shoe, it was a lot faster than she had remembered. Thank goodness her old dance teacher had told her how to get around problems like that. All she had to do was get up there, and never stop smiling—a smile could cover a lot of mistakes in tap dancing.

Flashing her thousand-watt smile at the mirror, Danielle started the record again and waited. Now how did it go? Something like step-shuffle-step-ball-shuffle . . .

Trying her best to find the beat, she struggled and huffed through the first part. It was hard work! Not even Danielle could smile when she was out of breath.

Danielle fell back on the bed, trying to catch her breath.

Tap dancing was definitely out! *So what was she going to do?* The contest was a little more than a week away!

She leapt up—an idea had come to her, out of the distant mists of her past. Baton twirling! When she was a kid, she and Lori used to spend hours in Lori's back yard pretending they were majorettes. That was before Danielle moved to Wood Hollow Hills, of course, but she thought she still had her baton somewhere.

It was in the bottom drawer of her dresser, way in the back behind the pajamas with bunnies on them, which she never wore but couldn't bear to get rid of.

Taking the baton in hand, Danielle gritted her teeth and began spinning it. Her wrist was pretty limber. The baton seemed to come alive in her hands.

Turning toward the mirror with a toothy majorette super-smile, Danielle's spirits lifted with every swirl of the silver baton. With a little rock 'n' roll music behind her, she might be able to do something very interesting in the talent competition.

She couldn't believe how great she was after all these years. Tossing the baton from hand to hand, it was as if she and the baton were one. She could just picture Teresa's face when she, Danielle Sharp, was named Miss Merivale Mall!

CRACK! One overzealous toss and the baton smashed straight into her mirror, cracking it in two, and smashing all her illusions along with it. "Oh, no!" cried Danielle.

So much for brilliant baton twirling. Danielle sank into the bed, her hands curled into tight fists. Now she had ruined her mirror, just because of the stupid Miss Merivale Mall contest—and stupid Teresa Woods!

Why did they have to have a talent section anyway? Wasn't the real talent being beautiful? After all, it was a *beauty* contest, not a *talent* contest! *What a farce!*

If the contest were fair, all she'd have to do was show up and accept the crown. So why did she have to go through all this other stuff?

Then, on top of it all, there was the "Interview." How incredibly stupid and humiliating! Danielle hadn't the slightest idea how to prepare for an onstage interview. Why, oh, why couldn't she have a coach like Teresa had? Why did her parents have to be so *cheap*?

Teresa's parents were out there rooting for her, helping her every step of the way. But Danielle's parents gave her no support at all—her father wouldn't give a dime to help her. No money, no encouragement, no nothing. And as far as her mother was concerned, the whole contest was ridiculous.

Well, what if it was? They were her parents, and they should be helping her!

Danielle sat up straight on the bed. Everyone was against her—except herself! She had to do something, right away, to swing the momentum in her favor. Something brilliant; something only Danielle Sharp could think of.

Going downstairs and hopping into her BMW, she drove off in the direction of Merivale Mall. Right then, what she needed was a clear head, and nothing cleared Danielle Sharp's head better than being at the mall.

"Look! There's Danielle Sharp! She's a finalist for Miss Merivale Mall! I just saw her picture!" Danielle saw a little girl about eight years old, jumping up and down and pointing at her as she stepped onto the third floor level of the mall.

The little girl's friend was excited too. She looked up at Danielle as if she were a movie star. "Wow!" she said in awe. "She's beautiful—"

Danielle caught her breath for a second, then flashed a smile in the girls' direction.

"Good luck, Danielle." The first girl giggled and called out with adoration in her voice. "We're rooting for you!"

"Because you're the prettiest one," her friend added shyly.

"Can we have your autograph?" asked the first girl, reaching in her book bag for a piece of paper and a pen. "Please?"

"Well, sure," Danielle answered as humbly as she could manage.

Danielle used the second girl's patent leather purse to write on. "Best Wishes, Danielle Sharp," she wrote in large script that slanted backward with dramatic flair.

A few other shoppers gathered around curiously. Across the mall others lifted their eyes in her direction. Suddenly Danielle felt as if she already was Miss Merivale Mall.

The first taste of celebrity was sweet. She could just see herself signing autographs for a big crowd of adoring well-wishers. What a hoot!

Smiling and waving to her new fans—who were holding their autographed papers as if they were priceless treasures, Danielle hurried away more determined than ever to succeed.

Those two girls were a sign from on high, she decided. A sign that she should give the contest everything that was in her. Danielle Sharp would be the *perfect* Miss Merivale Mall, and now she only had to convince the judges.

Danielle found herself making her way to the mall's executive offices, the headquarters for the pageant. Breezing through the front office, she called out to the receptionist, "Is Ms. Pierson still in?"

"Yes, she is. But it's almost time for us to go home. Do you have an appointment?" the receptionist asked.

"Oh, well, she told me to stop by—and here I am!" With that, and a smile, Danielle stepped straight into the pageant organizer's office.

"Hello, Ms. Pierson!" she called out happily to the stunned administrator, who looked up from the load of paperwork on her desk.

"Excuse me. You are—?" Glancing at Danielle over the top of her glasses, the woman did not seem amused.

"Oh! I'm Danielle—Danielle Sharp. Remember?" She smiled and held out her hand.

The woman looked at her hand as if it were a dead fish. "Oh, yes, Miss Sharp. I'm very busy, but can I help you?"

"Oh, yes, you've *got* to help me." Danielle flung herself into the chair at the side of Ms. Pierson's desk. It was time for the heavy guns, and even though she had never been in a play, nobody could turn on the emotions like Danielle.

"Ms. Pierson. I have a problem. You see, I am a very shy person, and every time I think of standing on the stage, answering those questions, I just freeze. And if I freeze, the day-care kids I work with will be so-o disappointed. I'm a role model for them—some of them look up to me as if I were their *mother*. If I get up there and blow it, it could seriously affect their emotional development." Danielle's face was a picture of humility and sweetness.

"Oh? And—?"

"So, if you could just, oh, I don't know—help me out. Like if I knew just a little bit about what kinds of questions they were going to ask—"

Almost imperceptibly, the woman's hands moved and folded themselves over the questions. Her eyes registered total horror. "Miss Sharp. The judges' questions are strictly confidential."

"Oh, yes! Of course! I know that. But, if I had just a general idea of what they might be—"

"Sorry, Miss Sharp. Now, if you'll excuse me?"

But when the woman stood up, Danielle seized her opportunity. Pretending to trip over her own ankle, she fell into the desk, sending the papers sprawling.

"Oh! I am so sorry!" she sputtered, bending down and reaching for the spilled papers. With a gasp of horror, the woman fell to her knees and began quickly gathering up the papers so that Danielle wouldn't be able to see anything she shouldn't.

But Danielle was one step ahead of her. Standing up, she made sure that her wrist pinned down to the desk the one piece of paper she really wanted. Now, with Ms. Pierson on her knees, Danielle let her eyes drift over to the writing on the paper the woman had tried to hide.

Sure enough, on the paper were two questions. Only one peek, and they were burned into Danielle's brain.

"I can't *tell* you how sorry I am," Danielle gushed, trying hard to contain the smile that was going to break out across her face. "Here, let me help you pick up this mess."

"I think you've done quite enough damage for one day, Miss Sharp," said Ms. Pierson, dusting off her skirt. "Please go at once. And the next time you want to see me, please ask for an appointment before you barge in here!"

Out in the hallway Danielle could have kissed herself. Even if Ms. Pierson did suspect she was up to no good, there was no way she could have proved it. Danielle had peeked at the questions for a fraction of a second.

Outside in the lot Danielle caught her breath as she rummaged through her snakeskin bag for a pencil. Finally she gave up and settled for an eyebrow pencil. She had to get the questions written down before they flew from her memory.

"How does Merivale Mall reflect the best qualities of American life?"

"What could people in Merivale do to make the community a better place in which to live?"

Danielle chuckled to herself. The questions were hard, but now she had lots of time to think up fantastic responses.

Getting into her car, she beamed at herself in

the rearview mirror. *Congrats, Miss Merivale Mall! Too bad, Teresa!*

She didn't feel guilty in the least. After all, she wasn't a professional improviser, was she? She didn't have a coach either. How was she supposed to do her best without a little help?

Besides, she was going to be super fair about the whole thing. She was going to give Teresa a chance to prepare too.

And wouldn't it be fantastic to be backstage at the Miss Merivale Mall contest, listening to Teresa Woods giving wonderful, brilliant answers—to the *wrong questions*!

CHAPTER NINE

The next day in the Atwood cafeteria Danielle made her way straight over to the table where Teresa always held court. It bothered her to see Heather there. Danielle knew that Heather was Teresa's friend first, and hers second, but still, it hurt. After all, Heather had said she was neutral.

"Hey, you guys!" Danielle called out as if they were still all best friends. Of course, they weren't. The Atwood Aristocracy had been shattered ever since the Miss Merivale Mall contest.

"Heather! You look fantastic!" Danielle said. "I love your hair! Who did it?"

Heather Barron looked a little confused. Then she reached for her tray. "Hi, Danielle. Thanks. It was Teresa's hair stylist, actually. Well, guys—I'm out of here," she announced sweetly.

"I don't want to get my hair singed when the sparks fly."

"Oh, come on. Don't be silly," replied Teresa. But Heather was already on her feet.

"Just kidding," Heather said, fibbing. "I have to check out a library book before my next class." With that, and a toss of her raven mane, Heather was gone.

"Mind if I sit here?" asked Danielle, her face a picture of openness and honesty.

"It's a free country—unfortunately," said Teresa, concentrating on her salad.

"Listen, Ter—I've been thinking," said Danielle, sitting down. "We shouldn't let a little thing like the Miss Merivale Mall contest come between us."

"Oh!" Danielle smiled as she watched Teresa trying to figure out what she was really up to. Because one thing was for sure—the Miss Merivale Mall contest *wasn't a* little thing. And they both knew it.

"Ter—" Danielle went on. "You and I have been friends for a long time now, ever since I got to Atwood, and I don't know about you, but I think we should *help* each other, not hurt each other.

"Like with the evening gown. I'm sorry I tried to find out what you were wearing. I was just dying of curiosity, that's all. And I couldn't just ask you directly, because we were fighting."

Teresa sat silently, taking in everything Danielle was saying. Danielle could tell she was starting to convince her.

"Can you forgive me? I don't know why I acted so awful!" Danielle opened her eyes very wide until they started to tear.

"I guess you were just afraid of losing." Teresa theorized sympathetically.

Gritting her teeth, Danielle sighed at this— the biggest insult of all. But never mind—she wasn't going to let Teresa Woods get to her. Danielle had a job to do, an important one.

"Maybe I was just afraid. Oh, isn't it all so exciting, Teresa. Both of us in the very same beauty pageant?" Danielle fluttered her lashes and smiled again. "The swimsuit, the gown, a chance to show off our talents— I mean, it's just soo-o much fun. I'm sure it'll be so close between us all the way—that is, of course, until they ask us the interview questions." Her eyes seemed to twinkle with secret satisfaction, and she let out a tiny laugh.

Teresa's eyebrows came together in a frown. "What do you mean?"

"Oh, nothing really. Nothing." She let that little giggle escape again, just to make sure Teresa had heard it.

The fish was going for the bait. As Danielle knew, Teresa's mind was devious enough to leap right to the truth.

"Danielle Sharp, do you know something about those questions?"

"Me? Know something? I don't know what you're talking about."

"I think you do. So, come on. Didn't you just say we should help each other, not hurt each other."

"Oh, darn! You're so perceptive!"

"So, what about the questions, Danielle? Are they really as tough as everybody thinks they're going to be?"

Danielle had to bite the inside of her mouth so she wouldn't laugh. "They're not too bad—" Danielle grimaced.

Teresa started twisting a napkin to shreds. "Well, what are they?"

"Well, I suppose—oh, okay. You asked for it. The first question is: How can Merivale Mall better help the teenagers of Merivale? And the second question is: Name *ten* reasons for shopping at Merivale Mall."

Teresa's face beamed. "They're easy! All I have to do is think about them. I can come up with the answers easy!"

"Well, it will be a lot easier than having to

make them up on the spot! Good luck—see you on stage!"

Danielle walked away trying to suppress the smile of victory that almost broke out on her lips. *And may the prettier girl win*, she muttered under her breath.

Now they were even.

"And how many atoms are there in the carbon tetrachloride molecule?"

Patsy Donovan heard Irving Zalaznick's voice through a dense fog. "Huh?" she asked.

"Patsy." Irv sighed and closed the book. "I can't help you study if you're not going to pay attention."

"Sorry, Irv," she said. "I just can't seem to get into studying today."

"I understand. I guess being a finalist in the pageant must be a heavy responsibility."

"Oh, Irv. I'm starting to feel really excited about it—even though I know Danielle Sharp or one of the other Atwood girls is going to win. But Lori showed me the gown she's making for me, and it's fantastic. And tonight, I'm going out on a date. Oh, how can I think about chem? It's impossible."

"Another date, huh?" Irv closed the chemistry book and put it aside. He cleared his throat and pushed his glasses back up on his nose.

"Okay. Punch me if I'm being nosy, but is it Bill Evans?"

"Him? No way!"

"So—um, who is it?"

"Oh, just Steve Kirkwood—"

"Steve Kirkwood— Oh." Steve Kirkwood's reputation reached even a guy like Irv. Everybody in school knew about the disc jockey of Merivale's popular teen radio show, "Perpetual Motion," and the effect he had on girls.

"I mean, I know I should study, but my brain has conked out or something. All of this is too much for me." Patsy put her pinky in her mouth and began to nibble her nail.

Shaking his head, Irving opened the chem book again. "Okay, here's what we're going to do." He pushed his glasses back up on his nose.

"*I'm* going to sit here and spew out everything in this book about fluorocarbons, and *you're* going to sit there and concentrate on what I'm saying. Don't let yourself think about Steve Kirkwood, or Bill Evans, or the whole bunch of guys that are after you these days. It may not be easy, but neither is an F in chem."

Patsy nodded. "You're right, Irv. As usual. So, go ahead—" A dreamy look came into her eyes.

"Okay. For starters, the carbon tetrachloride

molecule contains one carbon atom and four chloride atoms—see, tetra is the prefix for four. Patsy? Patsy?''

Irv's voice was drifting over her head like a fog now. To think that she, former fatty, Patsy Donovan, actually had a date that Friday night— with *the Steve Kirkwood!*

CHAPTER TEN

I can't believe it's me—I'm gorgeous! Blinking at the mirror, Patsy saw herself as if for the first time. Slender, shapely, and well, even Patsy had to admit it—she was *pretty*!

Her corduroy pants and suspenders were perfect—stylish, yet casual; comfortable, but still great looking. There was only one problem. How was she going to keep herself together until Steve showed up?

"Honey, would you like to eat something before you go to the movies?" Mrs. Donovan popped her head into Patsy's room on her way downstairs.

"No, thanks, Mom, I already had a salad."

"Maybe you'll inspire me to lose some weight, Patsy!" Mrs. Donovan laughed cheerfully. "Honey, I'm so proud of you. You really look your best.

It wouldn't surprise me a bit if they made you Miss Merivale Mall. You'd do the place proud."

"Thanks, Mom." Patsy glanced at the mirror again. That slender girl looking out at her from the mirror was a finalist in a beauty pageant, and she was somebody who was *popular*. She was going out with Steve Kirkwood. . . .

Ding-dong.

Patsy gulped. "Let me get it!"

Grabbing her jacket, she raced down the stairs, pausing for a second to catch her breath. *Oh, please, let this date go okay, don't let it bomb*, she prayed before she opened the door.

"Hi, Steve!" said Patsy. "Come on in."

"Hello, Patsy," Steve returned with a friendly smile.

"Steve, I'd like you to meet my mother and my little sister, Erica."

Patsy's mother nodded hello while Erica stared at Steve in wide-eyed amazement.

"That's Patsy's date?" said Erica. "Gosh, he's a real hunk!"

Patsy blushed all the way to the roots of her reddish brown hair, but Steve took ten-year-old Erica's comment in stride.

"Thanks," he said and laughed. Then, turning to Patsy's mother, Steve said, "Well, I guess we'd better take off, Mrs. Donovan."

"Have fun, you two." From the look her

mother shot her when she walked them to the door, Patsy could tell her mother was impressed. *Twice in one week too!*

Stepping out the door holding Steve Kirkwood's arm, Patsy felt as if she were flying. So far, so good.

He walked around the side of his black Toyota, and held the door open for her. *What a gentleman!* Patsy smiled and slid across the seat, her heart racing at ninety miles an hour.

Once inside, Steve flashed her another smile and patted the seat right next to him. "Why are you sitting way over there?" he challenged. "Come here."

"Well, I'm belted in and all—"

"Suit yourself. I hear you're a finalist in the Miss Merivale Mall contest," he said offhandedly, popping in a cassette of slow rock music. "Can't say I'm surprised. I always thought you were one of the best-looking girls around. Always."

Then why did he always ignore me? Patsy wondered. The feel of a hand on hers broke that thought. "Maybe later we can go down to the studio, and I can show you how I put 'Perpetual Motion' together," Steve was saying.

"That'd be fun," Patsy replied, relaxing into the ride. Even Steve's car was smooth.

The mall wasn't far from Patsy's house. Steve

pulled into a slot reserved for the handicapped. Patsy wanted to say something, but the lot wasn't very crowded, and Steve probably just hadn't noticed the sign.

"So, which movie would you like to see, Patsy? They're all pretty good."

"You've seen all of them?" she asked, surprised, when he opened the door for her.

"Well, not all. I haven't seen *Hotel Warriors*. But I heard it's great."

"You must really be into movies," Patsy commented. "Five out of six is pretty good."

Steve shrugged and threw her a wink. "Well, there are all these girls who want to go out with me, and I have to keep my listeners happy—"

"Oh." He was kidding. He had to be. Patsy's stomach jumped as they walked into the Sixplex. This was only her second date ever. She wasn't up to that kind of banter.

As if he had read her mind, he added, with a wink. "I'm just kidding. You know something, Patsy, your eyes are fantastic."

Whoa. What was it with this guy? Did he mean it, or was it just a line? Maybe Steve said that to all the girls he dated—but maybe he was being sincere. After all, Patsy never thought she'd get to be a finalist in the Miss Merivale Mall contest either.

"Hey! Look at that!" he cried when they

walked into the Sixplex. "*Hotel Warriors* starts in three minutes!"

As if it were all decided, Steve went to the ticket booth and bought two tickets. Patsy thought of telling him she'd already seen the movie, but she decided against it. Why make trouble?

Inside they settled into their seats as the lights began to dim. There, up on the screen, Patsy saw the same large hotel come into focus through a sharpshooter's viewfinder. There was the same ominous music as the credits rolled. Patsy was determined to give the movie another chance, but it was just too stupid.

Then, suddenly, she realized that she was leaning far to the right. Steve had pressed up close to her, so she had scooted over to have a little room. Next, his arm went around the back of her chair. That was okay. It was even pleasant, but when his hand started inching up toward her neck, Patsy felt her spine stiffen. He was acting as if they knew each other a lot better than they did.

Patsy tried to free herself without offending Steve. But Steve wasn't easily offended. A little at a time, he began pulling her toward him. Now he was nuzzling her ear with his nose and trying to kiss her neck!

"Hey! Wait a minute, Steve!" she whispered

as he began running his hand through her curls. "What are you doing!?"

"Just being friendly," he said in her ear. "I'm a friendly guy."

"But you're missing the movie," she said, giving him a little nudge.

"Movie? What movie? Who cares about the movie? Is that why we're together, so you could see a dumb movie like this? I'm disappointed in you, Patsy."

"Now wait a second, Steve. That isn't—"

Now he took her hand in his and stood up. "Let's get out of here, Pats. This movie's terrible anyway."

"I know—"

"Come on." He took her by the arm and led her out of the theater.

"Well—" He said he'd show her his studio, and she'd never been to a studio. And, after all, he hadn't really done anything that bad. He just tried to kiss her in a dark movie theater, and what was really wrong with that?

"Let's go," he urged.

"Okay," she agreed, still not feeling sure about leaving with him. "Are we going to your studio?"

"Not tonight. There's another show in there tonight," he said as they walked through the lot.

"I'd love to see a show in progress—"

"But it's such a great night. And I know a place with *great* views—" He opened the car door for her, then went around to the driver's seat.

"Okay." Patsy managed a weak smile. After a couple of minutes of silence, Patsy asked, "What's the name of the place, Steve?"

"Overlook Terrace," he murmured, speeding out of town in the direction of the hills.

Overlook Terrace! Patsy bolted in her seat. Overlook was *the* notorious "parking" spot in the county.

"Um, Steve, thanks for the compliment, but forget it, okay? This is our first date, you know? I don't think I'm ready for that," she cautioned him.

"What's the matter?" he asked, sounding a little hurt. "Don't you trust me?"

"No, it's not that!" Patsy said hurriedly, hoping she hadn't insulted him. "It's just . . ." What was she going to say now?

Of course, it *was* that—she *didn't* trust him, but how could she say it?

And so she said nothing, and neither did he for a while. They drove up Overlook Terrace and pulled to a stop on the side of the road. Even in the darkness, Patsy could see cars lining the shoulder of the road for a hundred yards ahead. *So, this is Overlook. . . .*

And there was Steve Kirkwood in the seat next to her, looking at her in *that way*. Too bad he was such a sleazy guy!

Just then, he reached over and drew her to him, kissing her right on the lips. Patsy felt herself tingle all over, just from his touch. But she didn't even *like* him! *This has got to stop right now*, said a voice inside her.

"Steve, take me home, please." Patsy's spine was straight and her tone was sure.

"Home? We just got here." He sounded annoyed and offended.

"Yes. I'd like to go home."

"Whoa, Patsy, relax. You're just too tense. Maybe being a Miss Merivale Mall finalist is getting to you." With that, he reached for her shoulders and began rubbing them. "Let me give you a massage."

Patsy drew away. "I mean it, Steve. I want to go home."

This time he believed her. "Fine," he huffed, turning the key in the ignition. "That's fine with me." His voice sounded like it was zero degrees.

They rode home in silence. But as he pulled into Patsy's driveway, he turned to her and said, "Listen, Patsy. No hard feelings, okay? Let's get together again real soon." Then, he grabbed her again and kissed her fully on the lips.

"Yeccchh!" said Patsy, closing the door behind her and wiping her mouth on her sleeve. "What a waste of time. Oh, Irv! Why didn't I just study with you?"

CHAPTER ELEVEN

Lori's heart jumped a little on Saturday when she heard Nick's voice at the top of the basement stairs.

"Nick! Hi!" Lori sat straight up; she'd been leaning over a large aluminum folding table. Scraps of material and spools of thread filled it with a rainbow of colors. In front of her was an open sewing machine, with a work in progress under the foot.

"Hope you don't mind me stopping by," Nick said, trotting down the steps. "I just wanted to make sure we were still on for after work, Lor. Eight-thirty, okay?"

Do I mind—? Having a terrific guy like Nick Hobart stopping by was one of the greatest things about Lori's life!

"Eight-thirty's good."

"Great. I'll come over to Tio's and get you."
Nick reached down and picked up a small swatch
of sheer peach fabric. "Terrific color. Are you
making something from this?"

"Well—" Walking to a closet, Lori pulled out
a peach chiffon dress and spread it on the table
for Nick's inspection. "It's for Patsy's evening
gown competition. I just finished it," she announced.

The dress had spaghetti straps, a form-fitting
bodice, and a skirt that seemed to float.

Nick let out a low whistle. "Impressive, Randall. That ought to bag her the title for sure."

"Thanks, *Hobart*," Lori replied, putting the
dress back in the closet and closing the door.
"Patsy's mother paid for the fabric, and Patsy
wants it to be a surprise for her at the contest.
It's a secret design. You're the only person,
except me and Patsy, who's seen it."

"Well, I don't know that much about fashion,
but it seems to me that this Mortenson guy is
going to be knocked out by your stuff." Nick
flashed her a special smile that said, "and I
knew it all along!"

What a sweetheart! thought Lori. On top of
everything else, Nick was a great friend.

"Thanks, Nick. I sure hope Mr. Mortenson
sees things the way you do. I can't believe I'll
be meeting him right after the contest!"

"Well, it's only a week now. By the way, I phoned for our tickets. It's first come first served, so we should be there early—at least by one o'clock—to get good seats."

"Okay." Lori looked over at him with a smile. "Pretty soon Merivale Mall's actually going to have a 'Miss' reigning over it."

"Yeah, I can just see Teresa Woods standing by the fountain with a crown on, tapping everybody with her little scepter—" he said. "By the way, how's Patsy holding up?"

"Oh, Nick. Would you believe she doesn't think she even has a chance?"

"Well, she is up against some heavy competition, Lori. Supposedly Teresa Woods hired a coach. And Ashley Shepard's costume was sewed by the same person who designs for the New York Ballet Company."

"Oh, I know all those girls are terrific, but still I think that Patsy has as good a chance as anyone—*if* only she had a little more confidence."

"She just lost all that weight—you'd think she'd be real confident."

"I know it sounds crazy, but sometimes I wonder if maybe Ann and I should have kept our mouths shut about Patsy losing weight, and getting into the contest. She's been under so much pressure lately, and instead of all this stuff making her happy, it's just seemed to be making her nuts—"

Just then Lori's mother popped open the basement door. "Honey, you have another visitor," she called down.

"I sure am popular all of a sudden." Lori laughed. "It's probably Ann or Patsy looking for a lift to work."

She walked over to the bottom of the stairs, just out of Nick's sight.

"Dani! Hi." It had been a long time since Lori's cousin had come by to visit.

At the bottom of the stairs Danielle drew Lori to her and planted a kiss on her cheek. "Oh, Lori, I've missed you so much!"

Lori breathed in a whiff of the exquisite perfume, and kissed her cousin's cheek. In spite of everything, it was always good to see Danielle. Danielle was so alive that when she entered a room, it felt like a party was about to start. Like most people, Lori was impressed by Danielle's charms.

But she had known her longer than most people too. And something told Lori her cousin was definitely up to something.

"Dani, Nick's here." Lori said it gingerly, hoping that her cousin's feelings wouldn't be hurt. A while back, Danielle had gone after Nick Hobart. But Nick was someone who definitely *was* immune to Danielle's charms.

"Oh! Hello, Nick," said Danielle, with a distinct pout. "How are you?"

Nick shifted uncomfortably. "I'm okay," he mumbled. "Well, Lori, I'd better be going, or I'll be late for work. Nice seeing you, Danielle." With that, he dropped a kiss on the top of Lori's head and bopped up the stairs, right past Lori's glamorous, wealthy, and slightly insulted cousin.

"He's sure in a hurry," Danielle muttered before she turned to Lori with an exasperated sigh. "Oh, Lori. I need help," she admitted. "And you're the only one who can help me."

Lori looked confused. "Help with what, Dani?"

"The Miss Merivale Mall contest! What else?" Lori was Danielle's last hope. Her parents had been a big washout in the support department, and she didn't even have any friends anymore—not since she and Teresa had started feuding.

"Well, I'd like to help if I could. Why don't you tell me what's the matter?"

Danielle and Lori settled themselves in chairs across the table from each other. "So far, I figure I have the swimsuit competition and the interview handled. They're going to be a piece of cake. As for the evening gown, well, my gown isn't perfect, but it isn't horrible either. If

I can knock the judges off their feet in the talent section, I won't have any problem winning."

"Well, that's terrific, Dani. Sounds like you have a *lot* going for you. But what are you going to do for your talent?"

Danielle threw her head into her hands miserably. "That's just it, Lori! I don't know! How am I going to knock them off their feet if I don't even know what I'm going to do yet? All the other finalists have something. Teresa has the piano, and Ashley Shepard has ballet—even Wendy Carter knows how to sing. But I don't have a clue about what to do. It's so-o depressing!

"First I thought I'd work up a soft-shoe routine from our old dance class, but it's been a long time since I practiced much. Then, I thought I could do some baton twirling. I was always pretty good at that, but twirling is so dumb."

Lori wasn't saying a word, but Danielle noticed that she was listening intently.

"So I was thinking maybe *you* could help me come up with something, Lori. You know me better than anyone."

"Well, what about singing, Danielle? You have a nice voice."

"Lori. You're forgetting. My voice may be nice, but I'm tone deaf."

Lori's brow wrinkled. "How about cooking?

When we were in Girl Scouts, you earned a cooking badge, didn't you?"

"Yes, but I haven't made anything since we moved to Wood Hollow Hills except toast."

"Well, what things do you really *like* to do? That's what you'll be best at."

"Let's see. I like to shop, I like to take bubble baths, I like to drive my BMW—oh, what else? Hmmm— Horseback riding is kind of fun, but I just started it."

"Wait a minute! What about math? You're super-talented at math, Dani!"

"Nobody is impressed by math, Lori. It's too easy."

Lori's eyes sparkled. "For *you* it's easy. But most of us have to struggle with it. You could do it like it was a game show on TV—with game-show music behind you. Or, maybe you could play out a little scene—solve a problem with some practical application."

"This sounds crazy, Lori—"

"Like, if you walked onto a bare set and said, 'I'd like to wallpaper this room, but I need to know how many square yards of paper I'll need.' Something like that."

Danielle considered the idea. "Hmmm— That would be fairly unique." *Unique, but boring,* she thought to herself.

"It would be unique! Those judges have seen

piano playing and dancing millions of times, but to see a math whiz in action—it'd make you seem so brainy, Danielle!"

"That's true—" But the last impression Danielle wanted to give people was that she was brainy. People got freaked out by it.

Lost in thought, Danielle found her eyes wandering over Lori's worktable. All this talk of the talent competition was making her head throb. "What are you making, Lori?"

"Oh, this is for my portfolio. They're all based on form and function—" Lori held up a burgundy jumpsuit and pointed to a sketch of the same outfit lying on the table.

"That's fantastic! What about these other pieces?"

"It's part of the same project." Lori beamed proudly. "I've got a chance to show my work to Mr. Mortenson of the Fashion Institute. He's one of the judges for the contest, and he promised to see me before he flies back to New York."

"That's great, Lori." It was too. Lori's designs had sure come a long way. They had a professional look to them now. Danielle couldn't help feeling a twinge of jealousy. She had always had better taste than Lori, but now . . .

"These things are fabulous, Lori." Danielle's gushing was sincere as she rummaged through the big rack next to Lori's worktable. "I *love* them!"

"Thanks. That means a lot coming from you."

"Can I try them on?"

Lori hesitated for a second, then shrugged. "I guess so. Just be careful, okay?"

"Oh, I will. Oo! I love this one too!" Danielle held up a dress with diagonal stripes.

"Well, help yourself. I've got to get ready for work. Need a lift anywhere?"

"No, I have my car." No way would Danielle ever be seen riding in Lori's used car.

"Well, I'll be back in a minute."

Lori would have never left the basement if she knew what was going to happen next.

Danielle stood up and stretched. That was when an idea took form in her mind—an awful, wonderful, and truly wicked idea. If the Miss Merivale judges thought *she* had designed these outfits, wouldn't they be impressed? She could pick out some terrific music to show them by, and, presto, instant talent!

Deep inside, Danielle knew her little idea had three things wrong with it. One, stealing Lori's designs was unethical. Two, it was dishonest. And three, it was low.

Her heart beating wildly, she looked over the outfits, one by one. What else could she do? If Teresa Woods was crowned Miss Merivale Mall,

Danielle would have to put up with her gloating for years! It was too humiliating to imagine! Besides, she'd find a way to make it up to Lori—somehow.

Holding up one of Lori's dresses, Danielle couldn't help smiling. It was smashing! Now, to put her cunning little plan to work.

"I've got to go, Dani!" Lori said from the top of the stairs a few minutes later.

"Oh, Lori, your outfits—you're going to kill me!"

Lori ran quickly down the stairs. "What happened?"

"I messed them up. I got lipstick on this one, and this zipper is stuck, and I pulled a thread on the tweed. Oh, Lori, I'm *so* sorry—"

Lori looked at her outfits in despair. "It's okay," she said, an edge to her voice. "There's no real damage. I'll take care of them."

"Well, I'm not going to let you," Danielle insisted. "*I* messed them up and *I'll* fix them. You work too hard for your money to spend it all on dry cleaning and tailors. I'll take the outfits with me, and I'll give them back as soon as they're ready."

"But I *need* them to show Mr. Mortenson in a week—the night of the contest, Danielle. You're too busy to take care of them. Besides, I can fix them myself."

"No, no, no! I'm taking them and that's that. I refuse to hear another word about it."

Danielle was up the stairs and out the door with the outfits before Lori could object further.

"Don't worry, Lori, I'll get them back to you as soon as I can!" she called from the top of the stairs.

Just as soon as I win the beauty contest, she added silently to herself. *Thanks a million, coz!*

CHAPTER TWELVE

Driving along the streets of Merivale with Nick, her portfolio on her lap, and a dab of cologne behind her ears, Lori was filled with a heady sense of anticipation.

That very day she would actually be meeting the man who could help her get into the Fashion Institute. She was scared but excited too. With all the work she'd put into her collection, Lori couldn't help feeling confident.

"I told Ann I'd meet her and Ron in front," Lori said to Nick as he dropped her off in front of the civic center.

"Then I'll go pick up the tickets and meet you," Nick replied with a smile.

The entrance to the civic center was swarming with people—friends, family members, and well-wishers. It looked as if the whole town had turned out for the Miss Merivale Mall contest.

Looking around, Lori didn't see Ann anywhere. She guessed they were running late.

As she was standing there, she heard a sneering voice cut through the other voices. "I'm telling you the girl was unbelievable. We spent the whole time in my car, you know what I mean?"

Lori turned around and spotted Steve Kirkwood leaning up against the wall talking to a group of snickering boys.

Lori turned away with a frozen stare and tried not to listen.

"She's a real hot tamale, all right," Bill Evans was saying now. "She kept saying, 'Kiss me, Bill, I'll die if you don't.' So I said, 'Cool out, Patsy. I mean, I know you like me and all, but let's take this step by step.' "

Patsy! Lori gulped. Her worst suspicions about the conversation behind her had just been confirmed. And what she was hearing was enough to make her blood run cold.

Now Steve Kirkwood chimed in again. "That's funny, Evans, with me, it was two steps at a time, know what I mean? I got in the car with her and she was all over me. The first thing she wanted to do was go up to Overlook. Then, when we got there, wow! She says, 'This is great, let's come here all the time—' "

"You got Patsy Donovan up to Overlook—at night?" Rick Anderson sounded shocked and amazed.

"*She* got *me* there, my man." Steve broke into a giggle, and the other boys followed suit.

How dare they! Lori turned around in disgust. That's when she noticed Irving Zalaznick standing close to the group. From the purple color on his cheeks, Irving had obviously been hearing the same lies. And, just as obviously, he didn't like them either.

"I *had* to take her there. She begged me. So I said, 'Okay Patsy, if you put it that way, what can I do?' "

This time the boys really cracked up. And Lori felt sick to her stomach. Obviously, those nitwits believed every word they were hearing. If something wasn't done about it, Patsy's reputation could be ruined forever!

Turning around again, Lori's eyes caught Irving's. Lori had never seen that look on his face before. He looked furious, and Lori thought she got a glimpse of something else too—determination.

Just then, Lori felt a tap on her shoulder. "Ann's inside, Lori," Nick was saying. Lori turned to follow him, looking back over her shoulder as they entered the hall. The last thing she saw was Irving Zalaznick walking up to Bill Evans and Steve Kirkwood with a maniacal gleam in his eye.

An excited buzz ran through the crowd as people filed into the lobby. Lori stopped and looked at Patsy's photo on display with the photos of the other contestants. Patsy looked fantastic!

"I can't believe what I just heard outside," she told Nick, but the buzz of the crowd made telling the whole story impossible. She'd have to fill him in later, and maybe they'd think of a way to clear Patsy's name. "Isn't that a great picture of Patsy?"

"All of them look good, but that's only because they have no competition."

"Huh?"

"Well, *you're* not in the contest—and you *know* you're the prettiest girl in Merivale." Nick put a proud arm around her shoulders and Lori blushed to the roots of her shimmering blond hair.

"Sure, sure, Hobart. Keep it up, flattery will get you everywhere."

In the lobby Lori saw Heather Barron, looking bored. Lori said hello, but Heather didn't answer. Maybe she didn't hear her—that's what Lori told herself anyway.

While Nick checked their coats, Lori scanned the crowd, looking for people with name tags. That meant they were judges—and Mr. Mortenson had to be one of them.

"Oh, Lori! Isn't this exciting!" Ann Larson walked up to her, looking pretty enough in her red cotton sweater to be a beauty contest winner herself. "Ron's inside. We decided to go in to get good seats. Hope that was okay."

"Terrific," Lori exclaimed as Nick returned. "Well, guys—shall we?"

It was just after they had settled into their seats that Lori turned and saw Irving slip silently into a seat behind them.

His nose was red and his eye was black, but he looked happy and deeply satisfied.

"Irv Zalaznick! Where did you get that black eye?"

Irv spoke softly when he answered. "Oh, hi, Lori. Hi, everyone. Is my eye black?"

"Yes, and blue," Ann gasped.

"What happened, Irv?" Nick wanted to know. "What's going on?"

"I just did what I had to do, that's all." From his pocket, Irv pulled out a pair of sunglasses and put them on. "Is that better?" he asked, unable to suppress a wicked little smile.

Just then the hall door opened to admit Bill
Evans and Steve Kirkwood. Lori could see in an
instant that they both had black eyes also—*two
each*!

They looked over and saw Irving and took
seats far away—in the last row. A group of
other kids saw them and started to giggle.

Amazing! Lori looked at Irving as if she had
never really seen him before. He looked almost
tough. She wondered if Patsy knew about this
other, daring side of Irving.

· Just then the lights went down and the sixteen-
piece orchestra began playing a medley of popular tunes as people took the last vacant seats
—late comers would have to stand.

From the back of the hall, eight judges filed
down the aisle to the front row. A jovial-looking
man with a mustache wore a tag that said "Professor Mortenson." *He looks sweet*, thought Lori.

"There he is!" she whispered excitedly.

"The Fashion Institute rep?" asked Ann, cran-
ing her neck.

"That's right. I'm supposed to show him my
stuff right after the contest. Danielle brought
everything—if she didn't forget, that is. . . ."

*I'm going to blow these girls out of the water
before they even get their feet wet*. Danielle had to
smile when she saw her image in the dressing-

room mirror. In her gorgeous white swimsuit, she was a vision—a redheaded beauty.

How lucky that the swimsuit parade was the first event of the evening. She'd be well into the lead right from the start, and everyone else would have to play catch-up.

"Danielle?" Fourteen-year-old Tracy Higgs poked her head in the door. "I put the outfits on the rack on the side of the stage. Maureen and Hillary are all dressed and ready too."

"Thanks, Tracy. I'm coming out now anyway, so I'll give everything a final check." Danielle had recruited Tracy and her friends as part of her talent ensemble. The three Atwood freshmen would be modeling the outfits that Danielle was showing in the pageant. *Lori's* outfits.

Walking backstage, Danielle saw some of the other contestants, milling around, trying to kill time and get a hold of their nerves. The sounds of the audience filling the hall added to the excitement.

Just then, a gasp came from a bunch of people standing on the other side of the backstage area.

Danielle craned her neck to see what was going on. From her dressing room, Teresa Woods had stepped backstage in a form-fitting powder blue swimsuit that was beyond "dynamite." Teresa looked smashing—her legs weren't skinny at all, they were lean and muscular. The Nautilus routine had obviously worked wonders on her.

With a gasp, Danielle turned away from her biggest competition. Teresa looked fantastic!

Oh, why did all this have to happen? Pouring a glass of water from the icy pitcher that had been put there for the contestants, Danielle was overcome with sadness. The whole rift with Teresa was like a bad dream! If only they could be friends again!

But, of course, that was out of the question. Teresa had done too many sneaky things. She had treated Danielle too shabbily. Danielle would never ever want to be her friend again.

Then why did she miss her so much? That was the worst part—missing Teresa. Danielle hated to admit it, but since their big blow-up, she had been lonely. Rat that she was, Teresa was fun to hang out with. Not only that, but when she lost Teresa, Danielle had lost Heather too. Heather had been loyal to Teresa in the end, not to her. Another cruel blow.

Waiting backstage for what seemed like hours, Danielle avoided Teresa's eyes and tried not to think about anything else upsetting. But it was all so unavoidable. There was Teresa, everywhere Danielle looked. Even though they weren't speaking, they still were painfully aware of each other.

A couple of times Danielle could just feel her former friend's eyes burning into her back—but no way was Danielle going to acknowledge her. That would be giving in.

Well, she'd just have to show them all. Danielle Sharp was going to win this contest hands down, and stick it in all their faces.

The pageant organizers were busy getting everyone ready. Finally the orchestra finished its medley, and Ms. Pierson called the contestants together.

"Okay, girls—" she began. "You all look lovely, but I thought I should run through a few rules and regulations before we begin."

Wendy Carter was nibbling a pink plastic fingernail. Ashley Shepard was twisting a silk scarf in her fingers. Teresa had a dazed look, and Danielle had to lean up against the wall so she could relax.

Patsy Donovan, a terry wrap around her, sat in a chair with a faraway look on her face. Her thoughts were someplace else.

"When your name is called for any event, line up on the X behind the back curtain. And remember, when you get onstage, never stop smiling.

"Also, please remember—as we rehearsed—just walk down the runway, turn, and come right back. Turn your head, so both sides of the audience can see you. You've got a lot of fans out there who want to see your shining faces. No lingering in front of the judges' seats, please—we don't want any traffic back-ups. So! Are you all ready, girls?"

A nervous buzz answered her. "Well, then, let's get this show on the road. Good luck, everyone!"

A drum roll announced the beginning of the swimsuit parade. Her heart beating, Danielle made a final check in the backstage mirror.

Danielle could just picture herself posing for the winner's photos in her swimsuit, with her new white pumps, a red ribbon across her chest.

"Danielle Sharp, you're next!" called Ms. Pierson.

Danielle lined up on the spot and the curtain parted for her entrance. The lights hit her eyes, blinding her, and suddenly, her knees were quivering. A definite no-no.

Taking a deep breath, she forced herself to put on a thousand-watt smile and begin her walk down the runway. "Never stop smiling"—it was terrific advice.

In an instant Danielle's shoulders straightened up proudly. *Why shouldn't I be proud? I look fabulous!* she told herself.

The audience obviously agreed. They were applauding wildly, and from the happy nods of approval the judges were giving her, Danielle could tell—she was on her way to victory!

CHAPTER THIRTEEN

The onstage interviews had just begun. All the girls were isolated so they couldn't hear the questions. They were standing around terrified.

Danielle couldn't help smiling. As confident as she had been about the swimsuit competition, she was even more confident about the onstage interview. Hadn't she answered the two questions a thousand times before, while looking into the mirror in her bathroom—her bedroom mirror was still out of commission from the baton hitting it.

"Mr. Ackers, judges, ladies and gentlemen," she was going to say when her turn came, "I think that Merivale Mall reflects the finest in American living because it's a place where people can find whatever pleases them in a free, tasteful environment. From the fountains to the atrium, the mall is there for everyone to enjoy. It gives us all a beautiful look at the unparalleled prosperity we enjoy in America." She had the answer memorized perfectly; she could say it in her sleep.

And the way she was going to say it was super. Her delivery was designed to be charming, fresh, and intelligent.

"Danielle Sharp—you're on!" Ms. Pierson's voice cut through Danielle's thoughts. She took a few deep breaths and strode confidently onto the stage.

There was Mr. Ackers, standing in a huge spotlight. Danielle stepped into the pool of light with him and smiled at the crowd.

"Well, hi there, Danielle," Ackers said breezily, reaching for her arm.

That's when the fright hit her. For all her acting ability in real life, Danielle had never had to speak onstage. Now, half the population of Merivale was looking at her, expecting her to wow them. It was one thing to parade around in front of thousands, knowing you looked like a million dollars, but to actually open your mouth and *speak!*

Suddenly the lights seemed awfully hot—so hot it was hard to concentrate. Her mouth felt as if it had a wad of cotton in it. Still, she smiled broadly while Mr. Ackers asked her the first question.

Danielle launched into her answer. But the words seemed to catch in her throat. She got them out finally, but they sounded so awkward and stiff—not at all the way she'd rehearsed them. Or rather, *just* as if she'd rehearsed them. She sounded anything but spontaneous. Ditto for question number two.

"Well, thank you, Danielle," Mr. Ackers mumbled when she was finished. "And now, may we have our next contestant." He seemed anxious to get rid of her!

Holding her head up as high as she could, Danielle stepped quickly off the stage. The audience broke out in a smattering of weak applause—applause that said: "Nice try. You lose."

It was the most horrible thing that had ever happened to her in her entire life!

Backstage, the stagehands looked embarrassed for her. One of the burly men who moved the sets raised his eyebrows and threw her a sympathetic look that confirmed her worst fears. "Nice answers, honey" he whispered consolingly.

Leaning against the wall, the crush of humiliation felt heavy. Danielle bit her lip and tried to keep the tears back. She still had the evening gown and talent sections to get through, and it would look pretty bad to have runny mascara all over her face.

"And, hello there, Teresa." Onstage, Danielle could hear Mr. Ackers greeting Teresa in his businessman's version of a slick announcer voice. She could listen to the other girls now that she was done. "Teresa, how does Merivale Mall reflect the best qualities of American life?" he asked, his voice turning somber all of a sudden.

Her heart in her mouth, Danielle moved to the edge of the stage, where she had the best possible view.

Teresa seemed to scan the audience as if she were looking for someone to help her out. Her coach, thought Danielle, straining her eyes to see Barbi's silhouette out in the crowd.

"Mr. Ackers," Teresa answered after couple of seconds, "Merivale Mall reflects the best qualities of our American life because—"

The silence was deafening.

Obviously, coach or no coach, Teresa's brains had turned to french fries when she stepped onstage. "Because it's beautifully designed, and it offers shoppers pleasant surroundings which in turn create prosperity for the whole community."

Not bad. Danielle winced. Even though the question wasn't the one she'd been expecting, Teresa had come through with flying colors.

"And, Teresa, what could the people of Merivale do to make the community a better place in which to live?"

This time Teresa seemed stumped. "Could you repeat the question please?" she asked.

As he did, Teresa began scanning the audience again. Danielle could see Barbi in the back waving wildly and mouthing words. Teresa squinted, bewildered, and then she answered, "To make the community a better place—um— well, we could plant more trees along the highways, I guess—"

The same sickeningly weak applause that had followed Danielle from the stage now followed Teresa.

Suppressing a giggle, Danielle hugged herself with relief. Teresa had just blown the onstage interview royally. On a scale from one to ten, Danielle might have rated a one, but Teresa's score had to be a triple zero—one for delivery, one for content, and one for total lack of poise.

But when her former friend stumbled backstage to the same humiliating hush, Danielle's happiness faded. Teresa looked utterly defeated, and nobody knew better than Danielle what that felt like. After all, she had just gone through the very same thing herself.

If everything hadn't been so awful between them, Danielle might have rushed up to her

friend and comforted her. Of course, that was
out of the question, especially after Danielle
had given her the wrong questions to study.

"And here we have Patsy," called Mr. Ackers
onstage. Danielle was about to go back to the
dressing area, but curiosity got the better of
her. *Might as well stick around for the entertain-
ment*, she told herself.

"Patsy, how does Merivale Mall reflect the
best qualities of American life?"

Patsy considered for a fraction of a second.
Then, she answered in a clear voice. "To me,
the mall reflects the best qualities because it's a
meeting place where people can come together
and pursue their happiness. It's almost like the
old town hall, but you can get everything you
need for modern living there too."

The audience and Mr. Ackers seemed pleased.

"Now, what do you think the people of
Merivale could do to make the community a
better place in which to live?"

Patsy didn't even have to think this time.
"We'd have a better community if people would
accept one another—if they'd look beyond the
surface and try to appreciate other people for
what they are inside."

When Patsy finished, enthusiastic applause
thundered through the hall.

Peeking out, Danielle could see the judges

nodding in approval. Mr. Ackers seemed impressed too.

Danielle leaned back against the wall and swallowed hard. Patsy Donovan—who really didn't look half bad in a swimsuit—had just taken a giant leap forward in the standings. That unbearable little nonentity was ruining everything! Because only one thing could be worse than losing the contest to Teresa Woods—and that was losing to Patsy Donovan!

Danielle could only hope the judges wouldn't let someone who used to be ridiculously fat become Miss Merivale Mall. It would be an embarrassment for the whole town. There *had* to be some sort of rule against it.

Oh, well, not to worry, she told herself. Patsy would certainly find some way to blow it. Even if her evening gown looked halfway decent, Patsy's excuse for a talent, whatever it might be, would be sure to sink her.

Ackers was leading the audience in a round of applause for all the finalists now. "But challenges still lie ahead for these young ladies," he was saying. "Because Miss Merivale Mall will not only have to look great, and be poised, she'll have to show her talents too! So on with the show!"

A drum roll followed while stagehands cleared the set.

Danielle saw Ashley Shepard stretching her long, lean, muscular legs. On the other side of the stage, Teresa was standing apart from the others, an otherworldly look on her face and a dog-eared copy of the music from "An American in Paris" by George Gershwin tucked under her arm.

Sybil Turner was called first. Her interpretation of "Strangers in the Night" was just flat enough to hurt everyone's ears. The applause that followed was an expression of sheer relief.

Next up was Ashley Shepard. In her little pink tutu, Ashley looked about ten years old. And when the music from *Swan Lake* began, her serious expression turned into a scowl. Her dancing was stiff and awkward. Ashley was trying too hard, and it showed.

Now it was Teresa's turn. She sat down at the piano, and the hall was instantly filled with lush, rich sound. Teresa's fingers deftly navigated the keyboard, making the most incredible music. Even Danielle was sort of sorry when the piece reached its conclusion.

The stunned audience held its applause for a fraction of a second before it burst out with its approval. Backstage, some of the other contestants and a few stagehands joined in.

Danielle forced herself to smile and clap so no one would be able to tell how sick she was really feeling. How was anybody ever going to remember Teresa's blown interview when she could play the piano like that?

"Danielle, are we on now?" Tracy Higgs's whisper startled Danielle.

"No," snapped Danielle. "We're after the chocolate-chip cookie." Confused, Tracy stepped back. Danielle seemed awfully upset and cranky.

Walking onto the stage looking svelte in a navy leotard and knee-length dance skirt, Patsy smiled brightly and signaled for her music to begin.

Backstage the sound man dropped a needle onto a rock 'n' roll record and Patsy took off. The aerobic routine she had put together with Ann's help was dazzling with its gymnastic twirls and kicks.

Leaping into the air with dynamic energy, Patsy was right on the beat. She'd been through the routine so many times that she could do it without worrying about the next step. Her enthusiasm was completely contagious. The audience couldn't help but clap along, and the judges were beaming and nodding their heads in time to the music. To everyone's amazement, Patsy Donovan was becoming a leading contender!

Her heart pounding, Danielle rushed over to Tracy Higgs and her friends to make sure they were ready. She'd just have to show Patsy up.

On the way to the rolling clothes pole, Danielle accidentally bumped into the table with the record player. A huge scratching noise filled the entire hall as the needle skated across the record. The audience gasped.

Luckily the soundman had stepped away and Danielle hurried away from the record player so that no one would know who had caused the accident.

Onstage, Patsy lost her balance and tripped. A soft moan passed over the audience.

The needle was quickly replaced, and the music resumed. But even though Patsy managed to get back on the beat, the damage had been done. Danielle could see the judges shaking their heads in sympathy.

Maybe her little run-in with the record player had been just what the doctor ordered, Danielle thought as she assembled her "collection" for the presentation. *After all, all's fair in love and war—and beauty contests!*

CHAPTER FOURTEEN

"And now, let's step into the world of fashion with our next Miss Merivale Mall contestant—Miss Danielle Sharp!" Mr. Ackers waved his hand and the lights dimmed in the auditorium.

A cassette was popped into the tape deck backstage and Danielle walked out into the light. With a nervous smile, she made her entrance.

She smiled broadly at the audience, took a few steps out to the apron of the stage, and twirled in front of the judges like a fashion model on her way over to the microphone. On the tape, soft samba music accompanied her every move.

"When I wear clothes, I like comfort and pizzazz! That's why I love this burgundy jumpsuit." Danielle's voice filled the auditorium with its sultry feminine tones.

In the audience Nick jabbed Lori in the ribs. "Hey, Lori. Isn't that one of the outfits you were just making?"

"It sure is," said Lori through gritted teeth. *How could Danielle do something so low?*

"When form and function come together, I'm happy. And here are three of my friends wearing some of my favorites. Come on out, girls," Danielle cooed. The three Atwood freshmen stepped onto the stage into three separate pools of light.

"These outfits are all original designs, and they're all handmade. They're designed for comfort and fun, from the pleated hips to the rows of jewelry sewn on the shoulders. Notice the pockets on this first dress—"

Danielle purred on as each Atwood freshman stepped forward to model. With the air of a great hostess, Danielle moved among the outfits, coolly noting the features of each.

"They're *all* mine. I designed every last outfit on that stage," Lori whispered hoarsely, grasping Nick's arm for support. "I can't believe what I'm seeing! Tell me this isn't happening. How can I show Mr. Mortenson those designs now? He'll think *I* stole them from *Danielle!*"

Lori could feel her face tightening. Her whole body was tense now. She wanted to punch her glamorous cousin right in the nose! It was all she could do to stop herself from leaping up on the stage and giving Danielle exactly what she deserved.

"I like simple lines, but ones that flatter the female figure. . . ." Danielle stood there smiling and pointing while her voice charmed the audience.

The judges kept bobbing their heads up and down in approval as they scribbled notes on their score sheets. Fashion designing was a unique talent, and Danielle's entire presentation was as refreshing as it was original. By the time it was over and the lights came on for intermission, everyone in the crowd knew Danielle Sharp was going to be hard to beat.

"Ooooo— I know a certain redhead who's going to be real sorry, real soon," Lori vowed angrily as she rose from her seat. "I'll meet you back here later, Nick. Right now I want to go see my cousin, so I can straighten this mess out."

"Go to it, Lori. Good luck." A quick peck on the cheek helped Lori to simmer down. But walking around the building to the backstage entrance, Lori grew heated again when she thought of her cousin acting as if she had designed and sewn those dresses all by her little lying self.

Danielle couldn't sew to save her life. If she ever tore a seam, she simply threw the outfit away. Lori knew that for a fact. Her own closet had quite a few items that were Danielle Sharp cast-offs.

So much for Danielle. This was one stunt she was not going to get away with!

"Lori! Hi!" Danielle flung her greeting breezily when she saw her cousin coming backstage through a group of well-wishers. She wasn't surprised to see that Lori was quivering with anger. It was only natural after all. But a few sweet words, a couple of "I'm sorrys" would handle everything, she was sure. Lori was a softy, always had been and always would be.

"Wasn't it great, Lori? They loved the clothes!" Danielle declared, moving to her cousin with open arms. There was nothing like a frontal assault to throw a person off balance.

"Danielle Sharp! How *could* you!?" Lori pulled Danielle away from the other contestants. "How could you be *so* dishonest?"

Danielle's eyes widened in disbelief. "But, Lori, what are you talking about? I thought you'd be so happy. I was such a *smash!*"

"Don't you play dumb with me, Dani! You know perfectly well what I'm talking about! Those were *my* designs you were just presenting!"

"But, Lori," Danielle rushed to explain, "you got it all wrong! I didn't say I *designed* those clothes—ever. I was just presenting them. That's all. That was my talent, not designing or sewing or anything."

"Don't give me a story, Danielle Sharp! You were cheating and you know it! Everybody out there has the impression that *you* designed those clothes! You ask anybody. And as far as I'm concerned, it's out-and-out cheating!"

"I think you're being too sensitive, Lor—" Danielle offered sympathetically. "I mean, I thought you'd be proud. That's why I used the clothes."

"Another lie!"

"It's not a lie, Lori. Honestly, I didn't mean to upset you in any way. If you want me to say I'm sorry—well, gosh—I really am sorry." Danielle let her eyes brim over with tears. She could always fix her mascara later.

"Save your breath, Dani. This time it isn't going to work. Here's the deal, either you come clean, or *I'm* going straight to the judges and tell them what happened! And I have photographs to *prove* what I'm saying too!"

Suddenly a quiver began to spread from Danielle's nose all over her face. Her cheeks and eyes turned bright red, and hot tears were filling her eyes—real ones, this time.

"Please don't tell," she begged suddenly. "I'll do anything you want, but please, *please* don't tell!" For once in her life, Danielle was totally sincere. In fact, she was more than a little desperate.

"No, Dani, I can't let you get away with this. It's cheating, and it's not right."

Now Danielle's chin was quivering along with the rest of her face. Danielle Sharp had to be the most pitiable beauty contestant ever.

"But if you tell, I'll be ruined. My whole life will be shattered. I'll be completely humiliated. She'll never let me live it down."

"Who?" asked Lori. "Who'll never let you live it down?"

"Teresa Woods," Danielle admitted. "She's always been better than me. Her family has a ton of money, and she's been all over the world, and her clothes are fantastic, and she has horses. . . ." Danielle's voice was broken and she could hardly go on.

"Are you saying you feel inferior—to Teresa Woods?" Lori asked incredulously, touching Danielle lightly on the arm.

"Of course I feel inferior to her," Danielle replied. "Because I *am* inferior, let's face it. Her family has tons more money—and she's more talented—and she's a member of the Polo Club. . . . And now the whole world is going to know I cheated! This contest proves just how inferior I really am. The only reason I even entered it was because I thought I had one thing that was better. And that was my looks. But now if she wins, I'll never live it down! I might as well go stick my head in a pail of cement!"

Danielle's tears were streaming now, and her words were punctuated with pitiful sobs.

"But, Dani, Teresa's your friend! Friendship isn't about all that stuff. Friendship's about accepting people, and liking them for who they are—not for how rich they are, or how talented they are."

"Easy for you to say," Danielle moaned. "You don't have to compete with your friends like I do. You're already superior to them. And now, I'm going to lose everything, every little shred of respect I've been able to get from my crowd."

Lori was silent, considering.

"You know it's the truth," Danielle went on. "Look at the way the guys on Nick's team tortured him when they found out he was dating you before the Atwood-Merivale game. You wouldn't want me to have to go through that—would you, Lori?"

Lori bit her lip, mulling it over. "All right, I won't tell the judges—on one condition—"

Danielle lifted her sad eyes toward her compassionate cousin.

"And that condition is that if you win the contest, *you* tell them yourself, privately."

"Okay. It's a deal." Danielle hiccupped and brushed a tear from her eye.

And a very good deal, too! she thought inwardly. If she won the contest, she would have proved to Teresa, once and for all, that she was prettier. The title itself wasn't important anyway.

Then, she could resign gracefully—tell the judges the truth, and tell her friends some story. . . . Maybe she'd say her mother made her drop out. Blaming your mother was definitely cool.

"Oh, thanks, Lori." Danielle sighed and gave her wonderful, forgiving cousin a grateful hug.

"Wait, a minute, Dani—not so fast. If you *don't* win, I want you to tell Professor Mortenson everything that happened. I want to use those designs, and I don't want there to be any question about who created them. Got it?"

"Lori, consider it done." That was easy enough. After all, once the contest was over, who cared what he thought anyway?

"Feeling better?" asked Danielle brightly. "I am."

Lori shook her head in amazement. "You're incredible, Danielle," she said. "How do you get over things so fast?"

But Danielle didn't get a chance to answer her. Because over Danielle's shoulder, Lori saw something that made her forget her anger, and everything else. Patsy Donovan was putting her coat on and heading for the door!

"Excuse me, Danielle." Lori dashed past her cousin and caught her friend by the gym bag slung over her shoulder. "What in the world are you doing?" she demanded.

"Just what you think I'm doing," replied Patsy, in a voice choked with tears. "I'm leaving. I'm through with this pageant, finished with all this phony baloney stuff!"

"What? Leaving the pageant? Don't you realize how great you've been doing? You can't quit now!"

But Patsy stared right back into her friend's astonished blue eyes. "I can't? Well, just watch me!"

CHAPTER FIFTEEN

"Patsy! No!" Lori lunged for Patsy before she reached the door.

Spinning around, Patsy glared at her friend. "Don't you dare try to stop me, Lori Randall! I'm gone! And you know the first thing I'm going to do when I get out that door! I'm going to find the biggest hot fudge sundae I can find and pour it down my throat so I can get back to being *me*."

"Patsy, you're freaking out. You don't know what you're saying!"

"Oh, yes, I do, Lori. This contest has made me realize something real important. Maybe I was lonely and sad when I was fat, but at least I was *myself*—not some puppet parading around onstage for a bunch of snobs."

Patsy was shaking with fury—a fury Lori had never seen in her old friend before.

"But, Patsy, when you got up there and talked about people accepting people, and how we've got to look inside people—the whole audience fell in *love* with you. If you walk out of here now, they're going to be let down in a big way!"

"Oh, please. Let's face it, Lori. The people who are out there rooting for me are the same people who used to treat me like I was a piece of dirt when I was fat. They're all a bunch of hypocrites as far as I'm concerned!"

"Hold on, Patsy," Lori urged. "What really happened? I still don't get where all this is coming from."

Patsy sighed wearily and took in her friend with her liquid hazel eyes. "Lori," she said, softer now, "when that needle skipped, something inside me just snapped. All of a sudden I had to stop, and I looked out at the audience, and they all had these adoring faces—

"And I thought, *where have all these people been all my life?* You remember how people used to ignore me, Lori? You remember how those jerks would make fun of me when I was heavy? You saw it all. No wonder I wasn't too happy.

"But suddenly I lose weight, and people want to be my friend, and guys like Bill Evans and Steve Kirkwood start buzzing around—guys who didn't even know I existed before."

Patsy let her shoulders drop. "Oh, Lori. Don't you see? All this attention, it's so phony. I don't want to be accepted because I'm thin, or because I look good in a bathing suit. I want to be accepted because I'm *me*—inside, where it counts."

Lori stared breathlessly at her friend. With all that out in the open, Patsy seemed a little more calm.

"Anyway, thanks for listening, Lori," she murmured with one hand on the doorknob. "Bye."

All the pieces were in place now. No wonder Patsy had been depressed in the face of all her new successes. Who wouldn't be if they thought it was all because of the way they looked?

"Not so fast, Donovan!" Lori cried. "You know what you need? One of these!"

Lori flung her arms around her friend and squeezed tight. "This is a good, old-fashioned hug. It's to tell you I think you're terrific—fat or skinny! And sure, there are some phonies out there, but you know what? They don't count! Only *you* count! You shouldn't walk away from your success because of them!"

"You call it success to win a contest because you look good in a bathing suit? Come on, Lori. You know better than that."

"Sure I do. But I also know that the winner of this contest gets a full scholarship, a new car, and a chance to get up and speak to people. If some airhead gets to be Miss Merivale Mall, that isn't going to do anybody any good, but if *you* make it, you'll be talking to school kids, and you'll really have a chance to influence them!"

Patsy wrinkled her face and considered. "Well, that's true—but I don't know—" She hedged. "I may not even win. I did trip— "

"Listen, you nut, I was out there with Ann, Ron, and Nick, and we saw the whole thing! When that needle jumped you recovered beautifully. I was so proud of you—we all were. Come on, Pats—we're out there rooting for you. Don't let us down!"

Suddenly, someone cleared his throat right behind Patsy.

"Ahem— For what it's worth, I agree."

"Irving Zalaznick!" Patsy exclaimed. "Why are you wearing sunglasses?"

"Oh, it's a long story. . . ." Irv's face was beet red and he seemed to be having a lot of trouble looking Patsy in the eye. In his navy jacket and striped tie, Irv was all dressed up, and he looked terrific.

"I just came backstage to wish you good luck for the rest of the contest. Your dance routine was super, Patsy. All your practicing really paid off."

"Thanks, Irv," Patsy replied. Then, impulsively, she grabbed his sunglasses and pulled them off his face. "I thought I saw a colored edge under there—what happened to your eye?!"

Irv shifted from foot to foot. "Well, it's a long story—"

Lori couldn't help herself. "He punched out Bill Evans and Steve Kirkwood when they started making up stories about you," she blurted out.

Patsy stared at her lab partner as if she had never really seen him before. And in a way, she hadn't.

"You did that for *me*?" she asked.

"Well, somebody had to," was his reply. "You don't go spreading stories about a great girl and expect to get away with it."

A great girl! That's when it hit Patsy—Irving Zalaznick, the guy she had spent hours with over a Bunsen burner, *liked* her—*romantically*!

"Uh, guys—I'd better get back to my seat," said Lori, who could spot something special happening. "Nick and the others are waiting for me."

"Sure, Lori. See you later," Patsy managed to answer. But her eyes were riveted on Irving.

Could it be that she hadn't seen him all that time because of his looks and his clothes? Was she, Patsy Donovan, guilty of the same kind of snobbery that she hated so much in everybody else? If so, that was all about to change!

Taking Irving in with new, unclouded eyes, Patsy could see that her lab partner really wasn't bad looking at all. Maybe he didn't look like a television star, but he did have nice sensitive blue eyes, and a sweet, crooked smile. . . .

"Irv, are you doing anything next Saturday night?" The words flew out of Patsy's mouth before she could stop them.

"Who, me?" Irv looked a little stunned and a lot happy. "No, not really."

"Well—um—would you like to go to the movies?" Patsy could hardly believe what she was saying.

"I'd love to!" Then a sly smile appeared on Irving's face. "Have you seen *Hotel Warriors* yet?"

Suddenly they both broke out giggling.

"By the way, Patsy, are you going somewhere?" He indicated Patsy's coat.

"Me? Oh!" she replied, almost surprised that she was wearing a coat. "Nah." She took it off. "Actually, I'd better get into my evening gown."

"And I'd better get back to my seat."

Suddenly, Patsy Donovan was feeling better than she had felt in ages.

*   *   *

When the evening gown parade began, Danielle lined up backstage with the rest of the contestants and tried to keep her cool. The contest was close, too close for comfort. Teresa's piano playing had been utterly and absolutely fantastic, but then, "her" design collection had really wowed them too.

It was important not to project confidence. The silvery gray gown she had finally found, in Snazzz! of all places, wasn't pink—but it was gorgeous.

"Miss Wendy Carter! Miss Marcia Ryder! Miss Veronica Bailey! Miss Teresa Woods!" One by one the girls' names were called out.

When Teresa's name was said, she shot Danielle a smug smile and walked onstage for the promenade. The pink satin dress was truly glorious and Teresa wore it like royalty.

"Miss Ashley Shepard!"

Fully recovered from her ballet fiasco, Ashley confidently strode across stage to join the other contestants. In her pale green gown, she looked like a southern belle of years past.

"Miss Danielle Sharp!"

Danielle raised her head and began walking to her marker on stage, but when she got there, Teresa was practically blocking the way! Danielle had to walk around her, and that made her appear less than a hundred percent poised.

Danielle smiled pleasantly as she stepped around her enemy, but all the while she was thinking about what a supreme rat Teresa Woods was!

"Miss Patsy Donovan!"

Danielle watched Patsy step gracefully onto the stage. There was something different about her somehow. Patsy seemed to glide across the stage like a young lady walking on air. The peach gown Lori had sewn for her was simple and unpretentious, but Patsy wore it like a princess. Danielle felt sick.

After all the contestants were assembled, Mr. Ackers stalled the audience while the judges conferred and made their final judgments.

Finally, a man in a tuxedo stood up, and passed an envelope to Mr. Ackers with a sly smile. The orchestra struck a dramatic chord, and every light in the auditorium flashed on.

"Ladies and gentlemen, I have the judges' decision in my hands."

"The third runner-up is—Miss Wendy Carter!"

Thank goodness! As Wendy went forward to accept a bouquet of white roses, Danielle breathed a sigh of relief. If her name had been called then, it would have been all over.

"The second runner-up is—Miss Veronica Bailey!"

That was a surprise. The Bailey girl had been

a complete nonentity as far as Danielle had been concerned. She was twenty years old, and her talent had been a totally boring violin solo.

"The first runner-up is—Ashley Shepard!"

Ashley was in shock. *And no wonder*, thought Danielle, *after that fiasco of a dance*. Ashley finally recovered enough to accept her white roses. With tears streaming from her eyes, she looked triumphantly back at Teresa and Danielle, as if to say "Ha! I came in second. But one of you is going home totally empty-handed!"

It was true. Only one of them would be chosen to be Miss Merivale Mall. Danielle smiled tensely and glanced over at Teresa. This was the moment they had been waiting for. *They have to pick me!* thought Danielle. *They just have to!*

A drum roll took everyone's breath away, and Mr. Ackers milked the moment for everything it was worth.

"Ladies and gentlemen," he finally began, fingering the envelope in his hand as if it were plutonium. "Would you all rise and greet our first reigning Miss Merivale Mall—MISS PATSY DONOVAN!"

CHAPTER SIXTEEN

"I can't believe it!" screamed Patsy as the crowd went wild and the other contestants rushed around to congratulate her, their wooden smiles hiding the agony inside.

Sending a big "thank you" in the general direction of the universe, Patsy couldn't stop smiling as the winner's sash was fastened at her hip. Just a little while ago she was going to walk out of the contest, and now—here she was—the winner!

The music swelled, and Patsy felt the soft brush of fur on her shoulders, as a red cape was thrust around her. Cameras flashed, and suddenly all the tension of the past weeks broke. Patsy couldn't stop the tears of relief that started streaming down her face.

In the audience, she spotted her mother, overcome by the same tears, and her father was beaming with pride. That scholarship would really help them out!

Then someone placed a sparkling tiara on her head and three dozen long-stemmed red, roses in her arms. Patsy began her walk down the runway.

Slowly, unsteadily at first, Patsy made her way down the aisle, the wild applause of the standing crowd all around her. She could see Lori and Ann jumping up and down, shrieking.

With a radiant smile, Patsy waved to the crowd and scanned the audience. Irving was there, all right, flashing her a thumbs-up signal. He had a goofy expression on his face, but he looked happy. And when Patsy caught his eye, she felt as if she'd never stop smiling.

"I can't believe this. I just can't believe it. . . ." muttered Danielle as she and the other losers were whisked off the stage. "I can't believe I didn't win!"

"I can't believe it!" screamed Teresa furiously as she burst backstage, kicking the dressing-room door as hard as she could.

"How *dare* they! How dare they exhibit such horrible, bad taste! To give the crown to that— that ugly, horrible, gauche— Ooooo, I could just die!"

"I know! Patsy Donovan, I mean—give me a break!" Danielle added, whipping a flower out of her hair and tossing it down onto her makeup table in the far corner of the room.

"By the way, Danielle," hissed Teresa, "that was a pretty cheap trip, trying to knock me down. Just because I outshone you in the talent section doesn't mean you had a right to knock me over onstage!"

"Knock *you* over? You were hogging the entire stage. You were practically standing on my marker."

"If it weren't for you sabotaging me, *Danielle*, I would have won for sure."

"Don't blame me, *Teresa*. You lost all on your own. Nobody could believe those interview answers you gave. I mean, talk about shallow—"

"Oh, right!" said Teresa, dripping with sarcasm. "That's because somebody, whose initials are D.S., gave me the *wrong questions*! Which reminds me—for someone who knew the questions in advance, it was awesome how you managed to screw up."

Danielle was speechless. It was true. They had *both* lost on their own! They had lost because of their answers.

Teresa wasn't through yet. "And that gown! I thought I threw it out last year— What did you do, fish it out of the garbage can?"

"Well, all I can say is, you looked pretty dumb out there in— What was that anyway, a swimsuit?"

"At least I can swim if I have to, which is more than I can say for you. And by the way, since when are you a clothing designer? How'd you get the nerve to make that up?"

"The same way you got the nerve to hire a coach."

"Don't make fun of my coach, Danielle. You could have used one yourself, you know. I may have lost, but at least I didn't look like an amateur."

"You lost with a coach, and I lost without one. So what's the difference?"

Growing tired of the fighting, Teresa changed tactics. "Ugh. Can you believe it? Patsy Donovan as Miss Merivale Mall? My poodle would have been a better choice!"

Danielle had to crack a smile. She couldn't help herself.

"I can't believe she won either. I mean, isn't there a rule about cookie heads and beauty pageants?"

A giggle burst from both of them now.

"You're much too kind. And that aerobic routine!" Teresa paused for a moment. "But then, the judges were probably thinking of this as a charity event. She needs the charity, heaven knows."

"Really." Danielle nodded enthusiastically. "I mean, isn't it ridiculous for us to get all bent out of shape about a stupid beauty contest? After all, there are more important things to worry about—like boys." *And friends*, she added silently, a rush of good feeling coursing through her.

"Yeah, and shopping!"

The two newfound old friends fell to the ground in a spasm of laughter.

"Danielle, you're a hoot. Why did we ever get involved in this anyway?"

"It was all your idea, Teresa!"

"Mine? How soon they forget."

"You know what, Teresa? The truth is, I missed you all this time."

"Yeah, well, I missed you too. Who else can make my life so miserable?"

"Did somebody call me?" Heather Barron had come into the dressing room and quietly moved toward them without their noticing.

"Heather! Hi!"

"Losing has done wonders for you two! I was wondering when you'd come to your senses."

The three friends came together in a spontaneous hug, and Danielle felt closer to them than she ever had.

"Come on, I'll treat you to dessert at L' Argent," murmured Heather, who could certainly afford it. "You can console yourselves with something wickedly chocolate."

"You're on!" said Danielle as Teresa started unzipping the back of her evening gown. "Thanks, Teresa—"

So what if she had lost the contest? Danielle had her friends back, and that was what really counted.

Danielle Sharp felt like anything but a loser. In fact, she thought she'd never stop smiling.